It's not my fault.

Self Discovery & Admission

Wendi Bear

Published by
Also I Hate Donuts

Copyright © 2013, Wendi Bear
All rights reserved. No part of this publication may be reproduced or transmitted in any form or by any means, electronic or mechanical, including photocopy, recording, or any information storage and retrieval system, without permission in writing from the copyright owner.
Cover Photography by Nicholas Iverson
Cover Art by B Designs Ink

ISBN: 978-0-9888997-3-5

Printed in the United States of America

This book is fiction. Names, characters, places and incidences are products of the author's imagination or are used fictitiously. Any resemblance to actual events, locations or people, living or dead is entirely coincidental. This book is not a memoir; it is a highly exaggerated piece of filth.
Shame on you for reading.

Follow the author online to see photos, new stories, current announcements and other garbage:

Electrikkiss.com

Facebook.com/Electrikkiss

Youtube.com/AlsoIHateDonuts

Funnyordie.com/electrikkiss

Twitter.com/Electrikkiss

*This book is dedicated to all the men
I have dated that treated me like shit.
Thanks, thanks a lot.
Without you, I wouldn't have been
inspired to write this piece of trash.*

Managing to have saved myself from being dumped after the drunken weekend with Donut, I was on cloud nine. I really thought that having made it through our first fight, things would finally start to get more serious. We continued to text back and forth every day.

Donut: You are so fucking hot. I want to be inside you so bad right now. Why can't you just let me pay you for sex?
Me: Because I already told you the fee, silly.
Donut: You did? How much?
Me: Just your love.
Donut: Ugh. Why don't you come by tomorrow night after work?

Now, let me confess, I wanted nothing more in the world than to see my little chocolate bar the next night. However, I had to play his game. So, I told him that I already had plans and then went out with a friend instead. To be cautious, I even deleted Donut's number out of my phone just to make sure I didn't accidentally drunk dial him.
 I foiled my own plan, though, by forgetting I had his email address still in my phone. Around two in the morning, after arriving home, I sent Donut some sexy pictures of myself.

The next morning I awoke to a text from my little honey bun:

Donut: Damn you and your sexy legs for teasing me.
Me: Good morning, Handsome. How are you doing? I wish I was waking up in bed next to you today.
Donut: I'm fucking hung-over. Listen, I have something funny to tell you.
Me: Shoot.
Donut: Last night, since you wouldn't come over, I invited this other girl I used to fuck. I was so drunk that when she got here I passed out. HAHAHAHA. When I woke up this morning she was gone.
Me: Wow! I'm going to have to think about that for a while.
Donut: What do you mean? I thought you would think that was funny.
Me: We agreed that you were to treat me as your girlfriend. I don't understand why you would think that I wanted to know about something like that.

Donut: But we laugh at fucked up shit all the time.
Me: Yah, but I want you.
Donut: I know. You're a goddess and the funnest girl ever but I just can't do it.
Me: Why? Why not? I don't understand! We have so much fun together and the sex is incredible.
Donut: I just can't be with someone who has small children. After breaking up with my ex (who had a young son) I made the decision not to get involved like that again.
Me: I am not your ex.
*Donut: *****, you need to be with a man who can support you, I just can't do that.*
Me: I don't need all that, I just want you, your hot body and you sexy cock.
Donut: Can you come by Thursday?
Me: Maybe, I'll think about it. I still have to decide if I will forgive you for last night.
Donut: Heh heh heh > :)

Table of Contents

Fire (Crotch) Bird 13
Lactation Olympics 15
Blood, Tears & Donuts 19
The Martini That Broke This Drunk Skank's Back 23
Giddyup Bubble Butt 29
What Is The Square Tit Of $8000? 33
Cliff Banger 37
Children Go To Hell 45
Ding Dong Ditch Em' 49
I'm A Dumb Slut Because Smart Whores Get Paid 53
Red Deer From Boston 59
Pirates & Dragons 63
A Dream Is A Wish Your Rotting Heart Makes 67
Tiny The Turkey 73
Jelly Belly Shelly 75
The Grossest Thing I Ever Did, Maybe 77
Baby Road Kill 81
Donuts Are A Girl's Best Friend 85
Talk About Being Stuck 87
Fungually Yours 89
Pretty Kitty 91
Date-a-Douche.Com 97
Donut's Sequined Slut 103
Cocaine: On A Cellular Level 105
My Four Leafed Stalker 109
Holiday Ho Down 113
Real Friends Help You Move Grenades 119
Somewhere Under The Rainbow 123
Skewer Through The Heart 125
That's The Spirit 131
Toys For Sale 135
All Dogs Go To Heaven, Even Retarded Ones 137
Caution: Razor Is Scented 141
Redbeard's Locker 151
Sausage Island 157
Unhappy Ending 161
Super Sandman & The Hand Gun 165
Liar, Liar Zipper On Fire 169
Dead Brothers Are No Fun At All 175
Bob Light Betty & The Mullet Man 179
Coke Who Res 183
Rockabilly's Are Stupid 187

Big Dick Mick: An Understatement	*191*
How I Lost My Virginity, Twice	*195*
CarniHELL: The Cruise	*199*
I Make Domestic Violence Funny	*207*
Piss & Shout	*213*
Demented Cheeto	*219*
Kitty, Kitty Gang Bang	*223*
Doctor Headlock	*231*
40's & Phone Balls	*237*
Mr. Personality	*241*
How I Shot Donut	*247*
Epilogue: Smart Whore	*251*
Acknowledgments	*255*

Fire (Crotch) Bird

I once dated a guy we shall call, "Stilts." This guy was a total douche bag. He drove a red sports car and thought himself to possess an awesome sense of humor among other delusional qualities.

Stilts used to joke about his "cool" car. He would say in what he thought to be an exaggerated porn star voice, "This car adds two inches to my penis."

The holidays were quickly approaching and I wanted to get Stilts something memorable for Christmas. So, I went to the mall and looked around for just the perfect gift. That's when I saw it. The license plate frame, engraving kiosk.

Ingenious!

With a smirk, I walked right up to the little teenage girl working the booth and asked her to engrave a license plate frame for me with Stilts (not so) famous quote. For the small fee of $18.50 she agreed.

I took my gem of a gift home, wrapped it and placed it under the tree.

The holiday had finally arrived. Stilts and my family gathered around the Christmas tree to share gifts.

That's when I did it. I gave my beautifully wrapped, deeply thought out, personalized present to my then love, Stilts. Uh huh, right in front of my entire family that he had just met for the first time.

He smiled as he excitedly opened his gift with everyone watching. Slowly, he removed the wrapping paper and peered at his present.

He was not laughing then. Actually, he never did put it on his car either.

Lactation Olympics

Early one evening, three years back, I tucked my kids in for the night. As soon as they were snug in their beds, I began the usual preparation of fat girl appetizers.

That's right, I took some prepackaged sausage ravioli and deep-fried it to perfection. I slapped it onto a plate and smothered it in Parmesan cheese. Beside it was a giant bowl of (my then husband) Beans' famous full fat ranch.

Fat girls can cook.

Next, I got out the rum, lime, mint and the rest of the mixings for mojitos. I muddled a giant pitcher and set it aside. With it were two big bottles of cub soda, to mix.

Tonight was a special night. My Who Res (Laverne and Tangerae') were on their way over along with our mutual male friend, Gonzo.

Laverne and I had both recently given birth to our sons. The two of us happened to be breast-feeding. Drinking alcohol caused our milk to come in three times faster than usual. This was quite the nuisance, especially because we couldn't give any of the alcohol filled milk to our tots.

We had to "pump and dump."

Right on time my Who Res' arrived, Gonzo was not far behind. We all headed out to my backyard to drink liquor, smoke cigarettes and make fun of Beans, per usual. We were drinking the mojitos pretty fast and I was getting sick of having to get up to refill everyone's glasses seven hundred times a minute. So, I brought out the pitcher. After setting it onto the patio table, I excused myself while I went inside to tinkle. I returned to my outside seat once my bladder was empty to discover it.

Milky mojito.

That's right. The fucking pitcher was WHITE!

"Have another mojito, *****!" Tangerae' suggested.
"Ya, let me fill up your glass!" Laverne offered.
I gave them both "the death stare." Despite speculation, I am not retarded.

"That was the last of the alcohol, Laverne. You 'ta-ta milk' destroyed the last of the booze? Are you serious? Go to the store, GO TO THE STORE NOW LAVERNE!" I was pissed.
Gonzo chirped in with a giant, perverted smile, "There's nothing wrong with this! Look, I'm building my immune system!" he said with a giant chug of the lactation potion.
This was not funny, it was a waste of good liquor.
"You are fucking disgusting Gonzo. Why don't you just suck on Laverne's tit?" I asked.
"Okay!" Gonzo jumped up excitedly.
"No way!" Laverne yelled in horror.
I had about all I could take of this shit. My booze was gone and the night was still young. So, I did what any angry, chest throbbing, nut job would do in a situation like this.
With cosmic force, I pulled out my left milk jug and squirted my "life juice" all over Laverne's ugly face. I smiled after seeking my revenge. My smile quickly turned into a frown because before I could even enjoy my success she got me.
That's right, Laverne had both her melons out faster than I could release a fart. They were going off like machine guns. Some even got into my eye, it burned like semen.
Gonzo loved this. Tangerae' was just drunk enough to be inquisitive. Uh huh, she was curious to know who could shoot the furthest distance. She reached down and grabbed a piece of sidewalk chalk. Then, she drew the start line.
"Ready, set, GO!" Tangerae' slurred.
Laverne and I whipped out our chest pistols, we gave it all we had.
Gonzo was growing an erection. I could see the little thing poking out of his pants as he ran under our milky streams with his tongue out.

I am proud to say, that even though Laverne mass produced four times the amount of tit juice I could, still I outshot that bitch two inches in distance.

I am a winner at Breast Milk Olympics.

In an attempt to "calm himself down," Gonzo made the beer run.

A few nights later, I was outside smoking a cigarette with Beans when he noticed some white, crusty stuff on the outside table. He was scraping it off with his thumbnail wondering aloud what it might be when I pulled out my swollen titty and squirted him right in the face with my warm milk.
Beans jumped like a pussy out of water.
"What the hell is wrong with you! Oh, my God! That is fucking disgusting! You are sick!"

I just laughed.

This became my new means of "Beans torture," for the three months I breast fed anyway. That's right, if Beans said anything I didn't like, all I had to do was release a teet and off he ran.

That was the only time in my life a man had ever run from them.

Blood, Tears & Donuts

I am going to write a little bit about my favorite thing in the world to think and talk about. This is probably the point you should stop reading if you happen to have a weak stomach. Right now, there is a huge smile on my face, sparkles in my eyes, butterflies in my stomach and....

RIGHT THERE!

Did you feel that? My little heart just skipped a beat. I am thinking about my sweet little Donut.

Let me tell you the first thing about Donut, he is a bisexual. Now, he is not the first bisexual I have ever dated but he is by far the most memorable. Bisexuals are confused and tortured souls who can only live by tormenting and crushing the hearts of the women who love them.

Seven years ago, Donut and I met on this little internet site you may or may not remember called, MyPlace. We chatted for a while online before going out on our first date.

Once Donut had finally planned our initial encounter, I drove to his place to meet him. I parked my car in the lot of his ghetto apartment complex.

Donut met me outside. When I first gazed upon his face, I noticed it to be all red and blotchy, like his whole body was blushing. He had that lack of charm usually only a ginger could possess and his hair was dyed black and slicked back with what may have been cooking grease. Covering his scrawny arms were what appeared to be "garage made" tattoos.

I was disappointed in my date to say the least but decided to get out of the car anyway. That's when I noticed it.

He was really short.

"Screw it, I'm already here," I thought to myself while giving him a smile and an uncomfortable hug.

Plus, he had bought me flowers. I'm a sucker for flowers.

Donut had actually planned a great date at a restaurant a city or two away. We ate amazing food, drank quite a few Martinis and he made me laugh with his awkwardness and uncomfortable bad jokes. The rest of the night is foggy, I can't remember most of the details.

The next morning I awoke naked in his bed. I was twenty four years old and a party gal who internet dated often. Needless to say, this wasn't a first for me. Being really hung over, I didn't want to deal with anything that day. So, I stayed and I drank some more. Actually, I didn't leave his love shack that entire weekend. After that, Donut and I became inseparable, for the six weeks it lasted anyway.

From that first date, our relationship blossomed. The two of us went to shows together, out to dinners, had kinky sex and adult toy store shopped. We confessed sins and fantasies, smiled and laughed. Constantly, we sent text messages back and forth. Before work we would hang out, on our lunch breaks and even after work.

One day Donut introduced me to his daughter. The three of us started spending time together, like a real family. His daughter liked me. Donut talked to me about us having a baby and living together. On Valentine's Day, he brought me flowers. I even told him that I loved him, he didn't say it back.

That's about the time it all happened.

One evening, roughly six weeks into our magical relationship from bisexual heaven, Donut decided to have a "guys only night." He informed me that his friends were coming over and I was not to come by. Donut had separated from his daughter's mom not long before meeting me and she hadn't allowed Donut to hang out with his friends. I knew that Donut was testing me.

No bother! I took the night for my own and went out on the town with my friend, Red. We met up with the Fun Girls.

Once the four of us had consumed enough liquor to kill a small herd (shortly after midnight) I headed home. Assuming that Donut's night was over as well, I texted him to say that I was stopping by his place for a goodnight kiss or something to that effect. I'm not really sure, I was pretty drunk.

The rest of the night is a huge blur.

Fast forward to that next morning:

I awoke alone in Donut's bed. He was sleeping on the couch. When I asked him what had happened, he refused to talk to me and instead told me to leave.

Immediately, I cried and I begged him for forgiveness. He just ignored my cries before throwing my pathetic ass out and locking the door behind me.

Then, he stopped talking to me all together.

I called him obsessively for days, texted, emailed, left desperate and pathetic voicemails, you name it. Donut never spoke to me again.

Well, not for a good year anyway.

This is what happened:

I showed up at his apartment that night after he had specifically told me not to. His friends were still there. He was trying to show off in front of them by treating me like shit, saying things such as, "I told you not to come here, you stupid whore!" then to his friends, "Can you believe this dumb slut?"

Next, he told me to leave while slamming his door in my face. I could hear him and his friends laughing at my expense inside his apartment.

Shocked and hurt, I ran to my car and cried. I sat inside for a few minutes and calmed myself down. After drying my tears, I returned to his door, knocked and asked to use his restroom.

He let me inside.

Once inside, I went into his bathroom, found his disposable razor, opened it up and slit my wrists.

When I arrived home that next morning, I saw that someone had thrown out my flowers.

The Martini That Broke This Drunk Skank's Back

So, what DID end the fling with my mullet sporting, retired, 80's pro-wrestler, boyfriend of sorts aka my Donut replacement?

First off, I must say that I officially broke it off with Brutus a few weeks prior to "the incident."

Secondly, he was not really a wrestler. He was the owner of a bar I lovingly refer to as the "Lit Fart." The title is as fittingly tasteless as he is, I assure you.

My oldest and dearest friend, Kitten came up with the bold description of this man upon first sight. To honor her inspiration, I shall call him, Brutus the Bar Owner Beefcake. Brutus, for short.

In the beginning, I did not have the same impression of Brutus as Kitten had. In fact, I thought he was a hot, beefy, stud muffin. I told him so in both text and email which he pretty much ignored along with all the nudie photos of myself I had sent him.

The last night Brutus spoke to me was the Saturday prior to Halloween. I had spent the day dressing up in a sexy wig and slutty costume before taking my kids out to Halloween events that evening.

I drank, a lot.

My son's dad, Mackey, was with us as designed driver. After the festivities, we arrived back to the house together and prepped the kids for bed.

Then, Mackey went home.

I still looked hot. So, I decided my night was just beginning. After all, why waste such a fabulous costume?

I did what any respectable and conservative mother of two would do. That's right, I left the kids with my grandma. Then I drove my buzzed, glitter shoe wearing, rippled tit and fake tanned ass over to the Lit Fart without a heads up to Brutus.

Knowing Brutus was throwing a big Halloween party, I did something, up until that fateful evening, I had never done before.

I showed up unannounced and intoxicated.

Once to the door, I paid the entrance fee and started a tab, something that Brutus never allowed me to do.

Why would he?

After all, he opens up the bar to all the girls who suck him off.

His staff did not recognize me due to the wig and costume. Once inside and still incognito, I headed to the bar for a cocktail before hitting the dance floor.

About an hour into my slutty dancing, I received an email from Brutus. He told me I should come down to the Lit Fart. Conviently, I could respond that I was already there. Brutus told me to come find him, he was "excited to see me."

I did as my mullet muffin instructed.

Once I found Brutus, he greeted me with a big smile before dragging me into the back room for five horrible minutes of one sided pleasure. I finished sucking him off before stumbling into the bathroom in an attempt to remove the red lipstick stains that were now covering my face. It was impossible, but I didn't care. Why, I was shit faced by then, anyway.

After I left the ladies room, Brutus informed me that he had a friend in from out of town and had to leave for the evening. Such a gentleman that guy, he opened the bar up for me before he left.

What a splendid idea!

That's about where my memory ends.

Flash forward to Sunday morning:

Mackey arrived to pick up our son for the day. I had about ten minutes until I had to leave for work. Awake, showered and dressed I suddenly came to the realization that my car wasn't there. With that, bits and pieces of the night before started flooding into my brain.

When I checked my phone, there was a text message from a strange number, "Are you OK?" it read.

"Yes. Who is this?" I asked in response.

"I drove you home last night, Falcon."

Suddenly, I remembered something, it was about getting out of Falcon's car in the early morning hours, wig in hand, before stumbling into the house. It had to do with scarfing down a corn dog in the bath tub, then passing out.

I ate a damn corn dog? Stupid, drunken munchies!

Mackey drove me to work that day. As he left, he told me he would stop by the Lit Fart on his way home to see if my car was there. A little while later he sent me a text message to inform me that my car was indeed still at the bar. Phew!

My car had four flat tires. Huh? That was strange.

I worked the day from hell. When it was finally over, Mackey returned to pick me up and drove me to the Lit Fart to retrieve my car. On the way, I texted Falcon to ask him if he had my missing car keys. He said he did and would meet us there. We all arrived at the Lit Fart roughly around the same time.

Together, the three of us inspected my tires. Luckily, for me they were deflated, not slashed. I thought that was pretty odd though Falcon did not. He noted my confusion.

"You don't remember what happened last night, do ya?" he asked me.

I shook my head in response. Corn dogs in the tub definitely didn't explain flat tires.

"Oh, wow. You came out here and got into your car to leave. One of them little girls from inside came running out after you. She tried to stop you from driving drunk," he explained.

"Oh, no!" I said. My guts started to turn. Already this was sounding familiar.

"She climbed into your passenger side. You were calling her all sorts of names," he continued, though I suddenly wished he'd stop.

GULP

"She reached into your ignition and took away your keys," Falcon paused for moment, "You punched her in the eye. I saw her this morning and she's got quite the shiner."

Holy shit.

A million thoughts were banging around in my foggy, hung-over head, guilt, embarrassment, fear, every emotion imaginable.

What was I going to say to Brutus? Not only that but how was I going to apologize for this? I've done some pretty messed up things before but I had never hit a girl, especially when she was trying to help me.

I am the biggest, drunken asshole that ever lived.

Then Falcon started again, "After you socked her she tried to run away. You chased her around the parking lot. That's when the boys working the bar came out and deflated your tires. I thought it would be best if I gave you a lift home."

I retract the previous statement, I am NOW the biggest drunken asshole that ever lived.

It took Brutus two days to respond to my emails. When he finally did reply, it was to let me know I was no longer welcome at the bar. I had already assumed that.

Falcon and I kept in contact the following week. As it turned out, he had also been working at the bar that night, as the bouncer. I couldn't figure out why Falcon had taken pity on me rather than had me arrested.

Well, until he asked me out on a date a few days later.

After the, "Get yourself some help and don't come back," "You messed with my business," and "My server doesn't want any apology from you and neither do I," email from Brutus, Falcon was kind enough to find out the name of the server whom I had assaulted.

Her name was Ruby.

I had to make amends with Ruby in some form, I felt horrible! I bought her a card and wrote, "I'm so sorry I hurt you. Thank you for helping me. I drank too much and am deeply ashamed of my actions."

Included was a gift, a lavishly wrapped makeup set. It was a "smokey eye" shadow pallet. I figured this way both of Ruby's eyes could match.

No! That's not really why, I'm not that bad.

My friend Pepper was kind enough to drop the gift off to Ruby for me. She took it to the Lit Fart that following Friday. I accompanied her. Like any self-hating, guilt-ridden psychopath, I hid in the passenger seat of her car while she made the delivery.

I am a coward.

Though Falcon said she had liked the gift, I never heard from Ruby again.

In retrospect, none of this really was even my fault. I mean, Brutus should have a sign posted somewhere that reads, "The Lit Fart, where you can beat off our owner but you can't beat our servers."

How else are dumb sluts going to know the rules?

I sent Brutus an email saying just that. He never did respond.

Douche.

Giddyup Bubble Butt

I was hanging out, guzzling a few beers a while back with my old friend, Tina. We were sitting on her porch one warm summer evening, enjoying the soft breeze. I smoked a cigarette as we had a round of filthy "girl talk."

The topic was Tina's vagina. You see, Tina continues to procreate with a man almost a decade younger than her. She is already a cougar, at thirty two.

"Sex with Drake is amazing!" she explained, "He's so young he goes for hours. Then, he can go a second round. It's so much better than sex with guys our own age."

Hmmmmmm, this got me thinking. I like sex a lot and I couldn't remember the last time I was with a man who could go for a round two.

Wait! My ex boyfriend, Morthos could go several rounds. That's right, I wondered how I had forgotten about that.

Morthos had been in his early twenties when we dated. Actually, Morthos was some of the best sex I had ever had. He didn't have a saggy old man ass either.

Just then, Drake walked by the window. He had a bubble butt. Immediately, I walked inside,"Hi, Drake," I said, "Do you have any single friends? You know, YOUR age?"

"Yeah, lots. Why?" he questioned.

"I want one."

Drake just laughed, "Let me think about who would be a good match for you and I'll set it up."

Perfect, I was in. I was going to score myself a long lasting, multiple rounding STUD!

That night I had wet dreams.

The next morning, I woke up and checked my phone. No new messages from Drake. What was taking him so long?

Stupid man.

I messaged Tina, "Where's my new young stud?"

She laughed, "Drake has been busy at work. I'll ask him who he thinks is a good match for you tonight, when he gets home."

This was not good enough for me. Did this bitch not know how excited I was? I was like a rapist in a woman's prison.

Pfft! Like I was going to wait another night? Please.

I decided that I better do what any impatient, psycho whore would do after being teased by calf meat. Once again, I used the powers of social media to achieve instant gratification.

Uh huh, I went onto a popular website and checked out Drake's "friends list." I sent friend requests to all the boys I thought were cute. Within a few hours, many of them had accepted my requests. As a matter of fact, one sexy little colt named, Spur, had even sent me a message.

"I accepted your friend request, but I'm so sorry, I can't figure out where I have met you," he wrote.

"We haven't met, yet. I'm friends with Drake's girlfriend, Tina. Drake was just telling me last night that he thought you might be single. He even said he thought you and I would be compatible and that we should meet," I lied.

"Wow, you are very pretty. I am flattered. I would love to meet you," Spur immediately responded.

"Great. Let's make a date," I suggested.

"Where would you like to go?"

"Do you live at home?" I asked.

Hey, he was twenty after all!

"No. I rent a room in a friend's apartment."

"Oh, perfect, your room will do."

Heh heh heh heh, I was in. I had roped my pony. He was twenty, I was thirty one. We had to meet at a coffee shop.

I texted Spur when I was on my way there that night and again after I merged onto the freeway. When I exited near his house, I messaged him a third time. Spur had still not responded.

I was only a block away when I decided to turn around. The final text I sent him read, "Going home now, Asshole. Thanks for flaking."

My phone rang immediately. It was Spur, I picked up.
"Yeah?"

"You didn't turn around did you? I'm sorry. My phone sucks. I just got all your messages at once, please come back. I'm at Starbucks waiting for you." Spur said, almost begging.

"I've heard that excuse before, Bub. I don't know I'm almost to the freeway. Besides, you might be a creep."

"Please, please come back!" he begged.

Aww, little baby needed his mama's tit. I loved this. Smiling to myself, I pulled up to the coffee house. There he was, freakin' adorable, yet still totally fuckable.

Meow.

"Parking is crap at my apartment complex. If you don't think I'm a creep I'll drive you there and you can leave your car here. I can bring you back after," Spur promised.

Pffft! Spur was so damn hot I would have sucked him off right there! But alas, he was still a sweet boy. The world had not corrupted him yet. He was not aware that giant whores like me even existed outside of porn. Shrugging, I climbed into his little car. It was obviously inherited from his dad, or maybe big sister.

Spur's apartment was just a block away. Once he'd parked, we got out and walked inside. His friends were sitting on the couch so I waved hello. They ignored me. Oh, right teenagers, too cool.

Spur shut his bedroom door. Then he put on a CD, John Myer.

Ewww. I hate John Myer.

"I hate John Myer," I told Spur.

"I'm so sorry!" he apologized, "I just moved in. It's my only CD. Maybe my roommates have something I can borrow. Let me go ask."

"No. It's cool, Spur. My attention won't be on the music anyway."

He blushed.

Then, he took off his pants. I slipped off my dress. I didn't think that he was sure what to do next. So, I helped him out.

That's right, I kissed him.

Spur penetrated me for two hours.

He was like a bucking bronco or a mechanical bull with a broken "off" button.

The first hour was quite pleasant. Spur was a hot treat on the eyes. He had soft skin with long, lean, tattooed calves and a beautiful face.

John Myer played on.

The second hour became redundant. I was thinking about the time and how I had to get home to my kids.

Plus, I was chafed.

Ugh.

John Myer continued.

That little cow needed to release his rope. So, I screamed louder. Next, I faked an orgasm. I told Spur how big his cock was. Finally, just as I was about to slap him in his face, he finished.

Once we were dressed Spur drove me back to my car. On the way, he started some small talk with me, "Sorry if I took too long."

"It's cool," I reassured him.

"My ex used to get mad at me for taking too long."

"I understand why. You are a little humping machine, like a rabbit."

Spur laughed before kissing me goodbye.

What a sweet kid. We never did hang out again, though we both tried. Spur still texts me on occasion. I repay him with topless pictures of myself.

Now, whenever I hear John Myer on the radio, I get a little wet.

What Is The Square Tit Of $8000?

The last few weeks I have been steadily riding the hormone roller coaster. Maybe "steadily" is not the best choice of wording. Last week I felt like a sardine in a shark tank. This week, thanks to the red river, I feel like a shark in a goldfish bowl. Stay out of my personal space or you will get bit.

I'm surprised by how much I hate men today, considering I can count the number of them I know and haven't slept with on one hand.

I'm a big whore.

Today though, I'm mostly mad at the man who gave me my botched boob job then (metaphorically) laughed in my face when I asked him to fix it.

It all started in May of 2010. I was twenty nine years old and had just finished several months of breast feeding my second child. My milk dried up and with it went my beautiful, perky C cups. I was left with two saggy pouches of skin I lovingly referred to as my "flat jacks."

So, I did what any self-aware, saggy tittied mother of two would do, I got a boob job.

I started by going online and researching doctors. Next, I attended several consultations with many different plastic surgeons. Eventually, I stumbled upon a doctor that just happened to be the nephew of the retired doctor who had done a friend's implants. His name was Dr. M. and that was good enough for me! Dr. M was not the cheapest, however, he talked the talk and made me feel comfortable.

I make horrible decisions when it comes to men, even when they are doctors.

Once my appointment date had been booked, I took out a loan to cover the costs and had my blood tests ran.

When my big day finally arrived, I was happier than a homeless man who'd found a twenty.

My friend, Fole picked me up that morning and took me to the surgery center. She waited until I was wheeled into the operating room to leave. Wishing me luck, she told me to call her when I was released and promised to pick me up and drive me home.

A little while after surgery, I awoke to a male nurse at my bedside reading my chart.

"How are you feeling?" he asked me.

"Okay," I said, "I need to call Fole."

He looked at me a little shocked, "Oh, dear. You already called Fole, Honey. You don't remember?"

"No......"

"Yes, you called her up about ten minutes ago. You told her you had rocket tits!" he exclaimed with a giggle before walking out of the room.

This was more embarrassing than waking up at the dentist's office with a boner. Fole confirmed this conversation on the ride home.

The next day I had a follow up appointment with Dr. M. He took off the bandages and checked the stitches. Everything looked great. Just as I was leaving his office, he stopped me, "Give me a high five!" he said as he held his palm up.

I looked at him confused.

"What? You don't remember high-fiving me after surgery yesterday?"

GULP

"When I checked on you in the recovery room, you told me I did a great job and high-fived me! Don't tell me that you don't remember?" he asked, laughing his ass off.

"Nope, and this is why I shouldn't drink either," I said before walking out the door.

A few months post-op, my left breast started to get hard. Not only was it firmer, but it also had started to hurt. I made another appointment with Dr. M. After an examination, he told me I had a capsular contracture and that massage would surely fix the problem. Not normal massage, I was to apply a horrific amount of pressure on this baby several times a day. Although it eventually did get softer, it became lumpy and the pain worsened.

After a year of dealing with the contracture, I noticed that the right breast had started to drop. Soon after that, I awoke early one morning and lookeded in the mirror. That is when I noticed them for the first time, ripples. My right breast was now rippled like an ocean current or a potato chip.

So, I did what any freaked out person coming to terms with the reality that their boob job was botched would do. I took pictures and sent them along with a letter to Dr. M. Also, I sent the same pictures to an attorney.

Dr. M saw me right away. He told me the ripples in righty were my fault for losing the rest of my baby weight. I reminded Dr. M that upon our original consultation, I had told him that I was on such a diet. His response at the time was, "Women statistically keep on ten pounds per child so you can expect to be twenty pounds heavier than you used to be." Not only did Dr. M ignore my reminder, he told me lefty was my fault too, because my body had rejected the implant, "We should definitely fix the contracture in your left breast. Have the ripples in your right breast been bothering you?"

Yup, Dr. M really asked me that.

Now, I don't know what planet Dr. M attained his medical license on, but here on earth tits are supposed to be round.

In that case, Dr. M would have been happy to fix both breasts for the small fee of $8000. That's just $2000 more than the original botched job and $4000 more than I had currently owed on my loan.

I again contacted my attorney. As it turned out, the shape of my breasts was not considered malpractice. This was because shapes are considered to be cosmetic. Maybe some people find lumpy, square, rippled hooters attractive. I wasn't sick from it, other people couldn't physically see the pain that lefty was causing and I was just a month shy of the two year medical malpractice deadline. In short, I didn't have a case.

To this day, my boobs are still messed up. If anyone should be feeling particularly generous…..Hint, hint.

Cliff Banger

I always seem to end up on the world's worst vacations. It is one of those "if it can go wrong it will" type of things. Also, I always end up sleeping with the world's biggest scum bags. Put these two things together, and you have a story about being isolated in hell with Satan.

Or as I call it:

A five (six) day trip to the Midwest to visit Cliff.

Cliff was unbelievably tall, close to seven feet, which is why I was stunned that his penis was so small. I had known him over a decade. The first time I saw Cliff again, I noticed right away that Mother Nature had treated him well. He had the same hair cut from back in the day with no signs of balding. His hair was naturally highlighted, long in the front, hanging over his eyes. It was just long enough for the boy band, pop star hair flip. Much like in his youth, he still dressed in all black, had baby blue eyes and a septum piercing.

Now, one major thing I have learned this year is what type of guy not to date. Never date a DJ. They are poor and will not pay for your dinner. Also, they usually carry coupons. This has been proven time and time again.

Secondly, because DJs are so poor they do not keep up on their oral hygiene. Do NOT let a DJ go down on you! You will end up with a yeast infection or worse, BV. If you get drunk and forget my advice, make sure you have a tub of plain yogurt in your fridge for emergencies.

I flew into the Midwest around ten o'clock at night on a Tuesday in late November. It was two days before my thirty first birthday. Knowing Cliff would be late, (DJ's are not very punctual) I told him my plane arrived at nine o'clock. After a half-hour of waiting in the snow, Cliff finally showed up. It was just after ten thirty.

Cliff was driving a car that I like to call the "rust boat." Upon arrival, he informed me that the passenger side door would not open. Instead, I had to ride in the back seat. I contemplated this for a moment then decided to climb my way to the passenger side through the driver's door instead.

The passenger door was held closed by a knotted bandanna. I was already beginning to question my decision about this particular vacation. However, I was calmed by the fact that we were heading out for dinner and drinks. At least nobody knew me in the Midwest, I wouldn't be recognized in the rust boat. Plus, the heater worked.

We pulled up to a popular pizza restaurant. Since Cliff is a vegan, we decided to share a few vegan items and ordered some red wine to go with our meal.

I thought it would be fun to "go vegan" on the trip for the experience. It wasn't just for the adventure, though. I knew Cliff wouldn't be paying for much so it would be cheaper if we just shared our meals.

After dinner, we headed back to Cliff's place. Stopping at the grocery store, we picked up a case of water, a few bottles of wine, cigarettes and I grabbed a huge container of plain yogurt.

We arrived at Cliff's place well past midnight. The two of us got drunk on wine, smoked a ton of cigarettes, had lots of sex and passed out just as the sun was starting to shine. It was mid-afternoon when we finally awoke.

Cliff asked me what I wanted to do that day. I told him that I didn't care, figuring we could just lay low. The following day we were checking into a hotel for two nights in celebration of my birthday.

Without other plans, we ended up going to lunch. Afterwards we spent the rest of the afternoon in bed watching movies, napping and having sex (this is my kind of vacation, anyway).

Around ten o'clock that evening there was a knock at the door. Cliff went down stairs to answer it. I fell asleep while waiting for him to return.

At roughly eleven thirty, Cliff woke me up apologizing for all the yelling. I was groggy and confused.

He told me that his friend, Amanda had come to his door, drunk, to see him. Amanda's boyfriend had driven her and was in the car outside when she knocked.

This is where his story got a little perplexing.

According to Cliff, Amanda wanted to come in and stay the night. That is when Cliff informed her I was there and she "flipped out."

Amanda confessed her love to Cliff, slapped him in his face and told him off for an hour and a half with her boyfriend still sitting in his idling car.

All I knew was that I had flown halfway across the country to get laid and have some damn child-free relaxation for my birthday. Who was Amanda again and how was she going to affect me getting my rocks off for three more days? Cliff assured me that the bitch would not have any impact on my trip. Comforted, I went back to sleep.

The next morning I awoke on my birthday to freshly falling snow. It was a beautiful and wondrous sight for this California girl. I put on my six inch, designer snow, ehh...hooker boots and my faux fur coat before heading out for a perfect photo opportunity.

In the meantime, Cliff loaded my luggage into the rust boat so we could sail off to le grande hotel for my big day!

After check-in and unpacking, Cliff and I headed out on the town. We walked down to an Indian restaurant for lunch. Cliff pointed out some of the city and was an all-around excellent tour guide. Plus, he looked really cute snuggled up in his winter coat, gloves and hat.

We drank a bottle of cheap champagne and had some laughs. Once we finished eating, we stumbled back to the hotel, arriving at about two o'clock in the afternoon.

Cliff had to head out for an hour or two to get "something done for work real fast" and would be back to take me to dinner and a club to celebrate. He told me I should take a hot bath and get ready in the meantime.

Once my spin master left, I did just that. As the "hour or two" passed and doubled, he never came back nor answered any of my calls. My text messages were also ignored.

It was around eight o'clock when I started to feel sorry for myself. I was trapped in a city alone on my birthday. With tears in my eyes, I went out for a cigarette of sorrow.

Delusionally, I was hoping to see Cliff walk up. At any minute, he would be on the stoop with flowers, a tub of yogurt and an apology. He'd be ready to take me on the town, somewhere exciting.

Unsurprisingly, Cliff never came. I met a group of drunken people my age smoking outside and butted into their conversation, hoping that they would let me hang out with them. They liked me! All but the bitch in the group. She wasn't having it and told me to screw off.

I eventually gave up on the evening. Feeling abandoned and defeated I stepped onto the elevator to head back to my room. That's when it happened.

The elevator stopped on the fourth floor and a hot, younger man in an expensive suit got on. He looked at me and smiled. Then, in an adorable British accent, he spoke, "Excuse me miss, but would you fancy a drink?"

Birthday crisis, averted.

My elevator angel was a New York City stock broker who was working on Wall Street. He was in town for one night to meet with a client. What luck?

Now, this is where I wish I could tell you that we fell in love and rode off into the sunset together. However, I can not. As I explained before, I only date scum bags.

Anyway, we spent the evening drinking champagne (on his tab at least) eating, laughing and we made out until the bars closed. Then, Wallstreet tried to get fresh with me. That is where the night should have ended.

He was drunk, annoying and persistent as he followed me to my room refusing to return back to his own. Though he was harmless, I wasn't in any danger, I was still really annoyed.

After sliding the key, I opened the door to my room and guess who was sitting there on the bed? That's right! Cliff had come back.

Wallstreet had not noticed Cliff's presence and followed me inside. Cliff looked at me, looked at Wallstreet, and asked if he should leave.

Now I was in a position of deciding which of the two men were of the greater evil. If I had any self-respect I would have called security and had both of them escorted out. I was drunk, and it was my birthday in a city of strangers, no less. I still wanted to have fun, God damn it!

Security showed up anyway as I was trying to push a very loud and drunken man out of my room at two o'clock in the morning.

Wallstreet eventually left. Of course that did not stop him from calling and texting me (non-stop for months but that's a different story).

Being heavily intoxicated and after everything that had happened, I was determined to get my rocks off. I used Cliff and his three inches of glory and did what I do best. I expelled horrendous, drunken lies and confessed all my love to him during penetration.

The next morning Cliff asked me if I remembered what I had vowed to him the night before. I said no, which was true, I didn't. Then I explained to Cliff about my problem with alcohol induced, compulsive lying. I am pretty sure he didn't believe me.

This leads us to my final day in the Midwest, or what should have been. Cliff left the hotel around eleven o'clock in the morning to attend his daughter's play. After the play, Cliff was to drop her with a sitter for the night before spending my last evening with me. He had promised to actually take me out somewhere before I left town (I did not hold my breath). Cliff said he would be back around three o'clock in the afternoon to join me in a now belated birthday dinner.

I enjoyed the day in my pajamas, ordered room service and watched TV alone in the hotel room.

Cliff never came back.

Not until after nine o'clock that night anyway. I should have strangled the jerk when he walked into the room but alas, it was my last night in town. I had already decided I would never see him again after this. Accordingly, I decided to let it go.

Cliff finally took me to my birthday dinner that night. Actually, to be more exact, I took him. He was broke. After eating, we loaded ourselves into the rust boat and headed out to the club. The club sucked, it was a dirty shit hole. Probably, I drank too much.

I looked at my phone to see that it was now midnight and time to head back to the hotel. Despite the putrid scenery, I was finally having some fun. At the last minute, I invited some of Cliff's friends back to the hotel to continue drinking with us.

The next morning I had to be at the airport by six thirty to catch an eight o'clock flight. I didn't care because I was going to stay up all night and sleep on the plane, like I used to when I was in my twenties.

By three in the morning, I was already over that idea and decided to have a little nap. At five o'clock my alarm went off. It was a quarter to six when I dragged my still drunken, hot mess of a self out of bed and started packing. I threw on some clothes, slapped on some mascara and started shaking Cliff awake. It was not working. Cliff was out cold.

I jumped on the bed, screamed, I even threw water on Cliff. Nothing was working, he continued snoring away. Still I was unsuccessful at waking him until a quarter after six. Once awake and stumbling, he went to retrieve the rust boat while I checked out of the hotel. I finished the procedure and I waited.

Cliff was not back with the boat until a quarter to seven. Frantically, I crawled my way across to the passenger side and ordered him to hurry. This was when Cliff informed me he was out of gas and that we had to stop.

We arrived at the airport at seven twenty eight. I grabbed my bag, without even saying goodbye to Cliff, and ran to the ticket counter. After handing the clerk my info
she leaned in and said, "Oh, you just missed your flight. See the clock? It's seven thirty one. We closed the gate at seven thirty. There isn't another plane I can book you on until tomorrow at the same time. Would you like me to go ahead and book that for you now?"

The floodgates were now open. Sobbing, I begged, "You can't make an exception for one minute? I missed it by sixty seconds! Please? You don't understand, I need to get out of here! I work tomorrow...and..."

UGH! I hate her.

After accepting my fate, I booked the flight for the following morning. Calling Cliff, he said that he would turn right around and be back to get me in five minutes. Two hours later, Cliff finally showed up. He took me to his house and then he left.

You see, Cliff had plans with friends that afternoon and Amanda was going so I was not invited. I begged Cliff to drop me somewhere, I asked if he had any friends who wanted company for the afternoon. Cliff had none, I sat on his bed all day, alone.

Glancing out the window, I noticed it had started to snow again. It didn't stop snowing all day and Cliff never came back.

Most boring day, ever.

By midnight, he still was not back. Frantically, I started calling and texting Cliff again. I begged him to come home soon because I couldn't miss my next flight. He understood, for the most part. It was one o'clock in the morning when he finally made it back.

Cliff actually woke up on time the following morning. I was relieved when he put my suitcase in his trunk and slammed it shut. When he turned over the rust boat's engine, I was impressed

We still had ample time to catch my flight, I was actually going to make it home today. I was clicking my heels in excitement. There was no place like home.

Just one tiny problem, the rust boat wasn't prepared for snow and water had frozen inside the driver's side door swelling the metal and it wouldn't close. Cliff tried slamming it repeatedly to no avail. I told him to just hold the damn thing shut and let's be off. That oral sex infection spreading jack-off refused. It took him ten minutes to figure out a way to rig the door shut with a bungee cord.

Oh, well. There was still time to catch my flight.
We were off!

The ground was covered in snow, the first big snow of the season and Cliff had not thought ahead. He hadn't installed snow tires nor chains onto the rust boat. We started skidding all over the road.

First, we swerved to the left, and then we skidded to the right. Cliff could not accelerate past eight miles per hour because of this but promised me that we would be okay once we got onto the interstate. We were headed in that direction.

Just one slighter problem, Cliff was out of gas yet again. Not only was I now worried about the time it was going to take to get to the gas station and to pump the gas but I was worried about how long it would take to un-rig and re-rig the door.

We pulled over at the first gas station and it was closed.

I hate Cliff.

Cliff forgot that it was now Sunday and in this particular city, places are closed to celebrate the Sabbath. He, being a poor DJ with bad credit, had no means to pay. You know, other than one dollar bills and some change. I had to use my credit card to pay for the gas. He said he would pay me back. I didn't hold my breath.

Eventually we made it on to the expressway and I caught my flight.

I never talked to Cliff again.

However, I did send him a drunken email one time that said something like this:

"Cliffff,.,,, youuu are tHe e biggest asshol eve in the whole fuckkking wOr ld! Like, everr!! ThE biggest one.! Thee ashol to end all asshol s s s!".

He never responded.

Douche.

Children Go To Hell

Growing up my family was very poor. My father could not hold down a job and my mother was working fifty-plus hours a week for a low wage trying to compensate.

Both my parents were alcoholics who dabbled in the drug world on occasion. They fought constantly. I saw things with my underage eyes that only refugees in third world countries have seen.

Living in a both verbally and physically abusive household led me to seek ways of emotional escape at a young age. The first attempt I made at finding a vice happened when I was only eleven years old.

My first vice was God.

My best friend, at the time, lived next door to me in the projects. Her name was Heaven. She and her family were active members in our local Lutheran church. Heaven was an obese girl who lived with her obese younger sister and her obese middle aged mom.

I do not remember the initial church invite, I just remember riding with them every Sunday to the little haven where all my new family ate, laughed, worshiped and rejoiced. Soon, I was attending more functions, like church activities and camps. It was nice to be somewhere without yelling and drinking, where people didn't call me names and hit me.

I attended my new sanctuary for roughly a year before it happened.

One night I arrived home from church feeling light with a smile on my face. I walked in the door and headed to the bathroom to soak in the tub when my mom stopped me. Her face and chest were puffy and red from her alcohol allergy.

With tears welling in her eyes, she said to me, "You need to help the family. Our fate is in your (eleven year old) hands. We cannot pay the rent this month, we are going to be evicted if you don't do something. When are you going to church again?"

GULP!

"There is a craft class on Wednesday night. We are making Easter Baskets and a pot...." I started to say, but she cut me off.
"Wednesday? Does the pastor like you?"
"I think so. He's nice to me."
"Good. Wednesday, you need to tell him you will be homeless unless he gives your family some donation money. I know those places make a killing on donations. Don't forget, if we lose the apartment it will be all your fault," with that she walked away.

Humbly, I escaped into the bath with an enormous weight riding on my tiny shoulders. How was I going to get my mom the rent money? We were going to be homeless if I didn't. I couldn't live with the guilt of making my family homeless. How embarrassing, if I brought my family to church what would my new friend's think of me? I pushed that thought right out of my head as quickly as it had entered. I learned very early in life not to care what people thought.

I needed a plan.

That following Wednesday I attended church already knowing what I had to do. Hopelessly, I tried to enjoy my time there but I couldn't. I was burdened down with guilt and trying to mentally prepare for the manipulation that lied ahead.

At the end of the night, Pastor John drove Heaven and me home. Once he pulled the car down our rotting, dimly lit street, I leaned up towards the front of the car and said to Heaven (who was sitting next to Pastor John), "This is probably the last time we will be driven home together. I'm really going to miss you."

Heaven turned her head around to face me. Confused, she asked, "Why? What do you mean?"

"My family is being evicted on Monday, right after Easter. We are going to be homeless because my dad lost his job and can't pay rent."

Pastor John was a holy man. There was no way he would ever let an eleven year old child and her family be homeless, especially around a holy day.

The pastor stopped the car. He waited for Heaven to get out before turning around to speak to me, "Tell your parents to attend our Easter Sunday service and I will make sure the church helps you with your rent."

With that I got out of the car and returned to my family's rescued apartment.

Easter morning arrived and my parents, delighted with the news, had everyone dress in their "holiday best." This usually meant my mother pulled the tags off of something new she had just bought, clipped a tie on my dad's shirt and pinned a plastic flower over a hole in a hand-me-down dress that I was given by a relative, but she had worn first.

My parents started the day with rounds of mimosas before piling my two brothers and me into our rusty old car. Before I knew it, we were heading off to my sanctuary. In the car they joked about having more wine at the church because it was the symbol of the blood of Christ. I quietly reminded them that this was not a Catholic church.

We arrived and I followed my family in, shamefully. My face was scarlet and hot with embarrassment. I sat through the sermon and cringed as I introduced my family to all my holy friends.

I knew that after this day, I could never go back.

At the end of the service, Pastor John took my parents into his office and presented them with a check. My mother took it like she was entitled, with a giant plastic smile. Pastor John told me that he added a little bit more money than my family needed, so that we could afford to buy holiday groceries.

I remember one last detail of that day. On the ride home, my mother said to my father, "Did you look at this check? I told Pastor John that we needed $500 to make rent. He said he put extra on there for groceries. This check is only for $525.

How frugal! What are we going to buy for $25? That won't feed us for the week, that won't even buy us dinner. I know the church could afford a lot more. He acted like he was doing us a huge favor. What a jerk!

Ding Dong Ditch Em'

When I was twenty six, I endured my first full term pregnancy. I also put on eighty pounds and acquired a mid-section festively decorated, as what I like to call, "the side of the left-over chunk of cheese that's been grated," aka covered in stretch marks. Oh, how I felt like an elephant. This was not a normal pregnancy, I incubated this kid for what seemed like two years.

Half way through my booze-less and cigarette-less torture I started finding other vices to get me through the days. My favorite thing to do was to pleasure my humpy-dumpy self while watching internet porn.

I was angry at the male species in general so the last thing I wanted to look at was a schlong. After all, that's what got me in this mess in the first place. Instead, I watched women masturbating, with devices, all kinds of devices. My favorite clip was of a woman using a glass dildo.

I had that page bookmarked.

Now, you may not understand what a task it was for me to masturbate in the first place. With a stomach resembling a hot air balloon and the inflated legs to match, I hadn't seen my hoo-hoo in months and I could barely reach it. I would sit down at my computer desk and manually lift up one leg up at a time just for access to my little bean. Removing them was just as much of a chore.

One afternoon, while finishing an uncomfortable love making session with myself, it happened!

DING!

There, on my computer screen, was notification of a new email. I clicked on the link and was directed to my inbox.

When I saw it my jaw dropped, releasing bits of the chewed up pastry treat I had been devouring.

There it was, an email from Donut.

I sat for a minute digesting this along with the remains of my Ding-Dong. It had been almost year since Donut had broken my heart and I hadn't stopped thinking about him on a daily basis. This pregnancy was pretty much his fault anyway, because it happened with my rebound guy while I was fantasizing about him.

My mind started racing, my pulse was pounding. I was so excited! He must have been emailing me to confess his undying love. See, I knew he had loved me all along. I bet we would get married now. Donut would adopt my baby and we would live happily ever after. With stars in my hopeful little eyes, I opened the email.

It read, "I jacked off today thinking about you. Not in love but in remembrance."

What the hell?

I read it again and again. Probably, I read it five hundred times. It still said the same thing.

What did this mean?

So, I did what any confused, bored out of her mind heffer would do in a situation like this. Uh huh, I forwarded the email to all of my friends asking for their advice. I don't remember any of them being really helpful.

After a few hours, I responded to my lemon bar, "I was at the super market yesterday. They were sampling out jars of mini sausages. I ate one and thought of you. Not in love but in remembrance."

Donut liked that, he saw a challenge. Immediately he emailed me back.

This continued on for a few days. My life was finally changing. Donut was coming back to me. We were going to have that family he talked about a year prior, his daughter and my son. It would be perfect!

Then, on the eve of the second day of flirting, I decided to disclose my little secret. That's right, I told Donut I was pregnant.

He never responded.

Well, not for another year anyway, but that's another story.

I'm A Dumb Slut Because Smart Whores Get Paid

In my most recent attempt to get over Donut, I stumbled upon the worst sex of my life. Brutus the Bar Owner Beef Cake. He was the only man I had ever dated that was unable to give me an orgasm. That is quite the accomplishment.

The first time I had sex with Brutus was in the back of his bar, in his liquor room, on a stool. You see, I told Brutus that I wasn't "that girl" and resisted his weenie for a good five encounters before this.

As it turns out, I was "that girl."

Brutus slipped his Jew stick in me that night for the first time. Three thrusts later, he pulled me off the stool and bent me over it instead. He spit on my ass and then stuck his half-soft, average sized Jewish peenie in my butt. A few more thrusts later, he pulled it back out and jerked himself off.

When it was all over, I removed a liquor wrapper from my dress and we walked back into the bar like nothing had happened. To Brutus nothing had, he does this all the time.

I whispered in his ear, "If you throw me out now I will cry." Brutus ignored me. So, I said it again, he still ignored me.

Then, he walked away and forgot I was even there. A half-hour or so later, I regained my composure and said my goodbye.

Now, wait a second. First, I must back up to the very beginning. I do not want you to think for a minute I was shocked by Brutus' brute behavior. After all, I knew he was a scumbag from the get-go. Just my type!

Brutus had a chiseled jaw, arms full of tattoos and the sexiest, highlighted mullet I had ever seen.

He was a guy I casually ran into around town for about a year and totally had "the hots" for. I knew he had "the hots" for me too. There was chemistry, a spark, or, maybe it was just because he always comp'd out my tab when I was hanging at his bar.

The first time I walked into the Lit Fart alone he immediately noticed and started flirting with me. Brutus invited me to the patio for drinks and introduced me to his friends before asking me to stay until closing.

I did and after closing, I drove us to another bar for some more drinks. Around two in the morning I took Brutus back to the Lit Fart.

That's when it happened, Brutus went for It. I do not mean he went for a kiss either. He literally grabbed the back of my head, pushed my face into his crotch and tried to get me to give him a blow job right there. I was so disappointed, I let out a huge sigh and said, "Ahhh, man! Really? Sorry, Buddy. Find someone else to blow you, I'm not 'that girl.'"

I thought to myself, "Man THIS sucks! A guy I'm into and he's one of those? Ugh!"

Brutus spent the rest of our relationship (?) trying to prove to me he wasn't just in it for the sex. He failed horribly.

At least a week from my first sexual encounter with Brutus came and went without a word from him. I wrote a horrible email calling him all sorts of names. At the last second I didn't send it. Instead, I sent him a two word text, "Game over?"

Within minutes, my phone rang. It was Brutus. He apologized for not calling and told me he wanted to see me again.

We continued to see each other for a couple months, roughly once a week. Every time we saw each other, it was pretty much the same thing. I would show up at his bar and we would leave to grab dinner, sometimes we wouldn't. Either way, we always ended up bottomless back at his bar after closing or in my car. He would pull out his semi-hard Jew dog and either insert it into my butt or into my mouth for a few thrusts and then jerk himself off while I played with his matzo-balls.

Eventually, I started complaining.

One night in my car, in the parking lot of a restaurant we had just finished eating a very late dinner at, Brutus pulled his pants down as so I could work off my meal.

I asked half way through this particular blow job if I could straddle him. With an annoyed grunt, he obliged me. Once I was on top, I could feel my 80's Wrestler losing his *A-hemmm* "function."

I told myself to just ride that pony. Up until this point in my life, I could always manage to squeeze out an orgasm in a minute's time this way.

To hurry myself up I asked Brutus to talk dirty to me. This is what he said, "Do you like my cock in your mouth, baby? You wanna' suck my big cock? Do you want me to fuck your face?"

That's where I gave up. I got off (of him), fingered his furry asshole and licked his sweaty, sour matzo-balls while he jacked himself off again.

I didn't see Brutus for about three weeks after that. When we finally met up, it was at an actual restaurant and not his bar. That is where it finally happened, Brutus invited me to his house.

I was shocked.

You see, every time before this one night, I had gone out of my way to pamper. I shaved my girl parts, wore cute lingerie and did all the things I could do to prepare for the night ahead. This particular night, I had just started my period and had decided I wasn't going to lick anything. That's right, I was going to get my dinner and bail.

Now, none of my lack of pampering mattered. I had to go out of curiosity alone. Countless days and nights, I had spent thinking and discussing with my girl-friends all the different scenarios of why he had not taken me there before and what he must be hiding. I was intrigued, was I going to find out that he had a wife? Did he really live in a swamp? What if he had a real-life wrestling ring in his living room?

After dinner, I followed Brutus home. Halfway to his house he cut another car off on the freeway exiting at the last minute and lost me. I pulled into a gas station and called his cell phone. He gave me his address and I made it there, eventually.

Brutus had now earned himself ample time to prepare for my arrival. One would think maybe he would put on some music, do some quick cleanup, pour me a drink, change his sheets, or perhaps even shower.

Nope, he didn't do any of that.

Actually, his house was a wreck. It stunk like dog. He had three nasty, yelpy, little dogs running around and barely noticed I was there once I had arrived. Brutus was walking around his house with his attention on everything except me.

I didn't care because I was gonna' get some.

Uh huh, I was finally going to get real sex in an actual bed. Why, I hadn't gotten off since Donut.

I explained to Brutus that I was on my period and asked to take a quick shower. Once in the bathroom, I removed my little cotton friend and washed off. After, I put a towel down on his dog hair and drool ridden bed.

I was ready for action.

Brutus immediately offered me a back rub. He had been telling me since the beginning that he was the best at back rubs. After putting on some strange Italian opera music (the kind my ex father in law used to play), he stripped down and instructed me to lie on my stomach while he placed his hands on my ass. Then, Brutus began annoyingly squeezing my cheeks while asking me, "Do you like that? Ya? You like me squeezing your ass?"

So, I lied, "Uhhhh, ya?" I was gonna' get some.

Brutus then began lightly squeezing my back in fast, tickling motions. I don't know what the hell he was doing but it wasn't massage. He pulled me up to a sitting position and then started fucking my tits. This was getting him close to the finish line. There was no way was I going to let that happen.

"Uh, wait, aren't we gonna'...I mean, I had wanted to.. WHAT ABOUT ME?" I finally screamed.

Brutus looked at me confused, "What? You keep saying that, but I don't know what you want."

"I want to you to make love to me," I said.

BLOOP! Erection completely eradicated.

"Sigh, listen, I'll have you here again this week, okay? We will do this again this week," he promised.

Brutus got up and started fussing with his stinky dogs. I made mention of the smell which really angered him. He put the dogs on the bed and was making baby talk to them. Deciding that one was getting out of hand, he put it outside his bedroom door. It whimpered and he let it back in. Brutus then decided the dog was getting out of hand again so he locked it out into the backyard.

Then he turned on the sports channel.

I was uncomfortable and debating on whether or not I should leave. The bed was disgusting and watching Brutus tongue his dogs was even more disturbing. When I started to speak he cut me off, asking, "Don't you ever just stop talking?"

Before I could even reply, he was up again checking this, doing that. He went into the backyard to check on his dog and noticed his gate was open. Brutus went on a dog hunt.

When he returned I was dressed and said my goodbye. I drove home disgusted and thoroughly disappointed. The smell of dirty dog lingered on me for days. That's about where our relationship (?) ended.

Or, more like, where it should have ended. We had "the talk" via text message a few days later.

Two more days went by. I received a new message from Brutus. It said, "Do you want to come down to the Lit Fart for some meaningless sex? I'll make you get off hard!"

I replied, "Of course I do. Be there in an hour."

Now, do you want to tell me how this night ended?

Yup! You guessed it!

The three B's:
1. Butt
2. B.J.
3. Balls

This time, though, Brutus added an extra insult to injury. Right in the middle of it all, he asked when my last STI test was. I replied, "I can't remember……the guy I dated before you is a bisexual."

Brutus finished himself off anyway.

Five minutes later, I was walked out to my car completely unsatisfied and ashamed, as usual.

In retrospect, if I had any brain at all, I would have told Brutus from the get-go, "Brutus, here is my bank account number, *********. Put in the amount you think I am worth. If I like it, I will come down to that damn Lit Fart once a week, do whatever you want, and leave without talking. You won't even have to buy me dinner. Just make that deposit once a month and everything will be fine."

But I'm not smart like a whore. I'm a dumb slut.

Red Deer From Boston

In my mid-twenties, I drank a lot. Most often my partner in crime was Red. Much like myself at the time, Red wore a size 12 and walked around a bit swollen in the face from the over consumption of alcohol. Also like me, she had fabulous shoes! Where I was a platinum blonde mess, she was red, with short curls that belonged in a Broadway play or perhaps a comic strip.

Unlike me, Red could hold her liquor. At any given point in time, regardless of what or how much Red consumed, she could put on a straight face and fool anyone into believing she was a perfectly square and innocent, designated driver. This came in handy often. Especially when I was skipping around intoxicated, naked and out of control in public, pissing on anything I could find. You may think I am exaggerating the point but this time, I am not.

Red and I were not always alone in our chaos creating, we also ran in a pack, the self-proclaimed "Fun Girls."

After one seafood eating, seventeen margarita drinking lunch (on a hangover) with Red, she invited me to a MME wrestling match. Her brother and his friends had an extra ticket and I gleefully accepted their amazing offer. Looking back, this may very well be where my mullet obsession all began.

Once we arrived at the match, we were seated next to some random tall bombshell. She was wearing jeans and a baseball jersey. Her long brown, wavy hair almost reached her AHSSS. Turned out, she was our age or maybe a year or two younger.

Red and I introduced ourselves, her name was Bahssten. We found out that she was new to California. She had just moved from the East Coast to attend grad school and had been dating Red's, brother's friend. Other than these boys, she didn't know anyone in the state. After a few minutes of conversation with Bahssten, Red and I discovered we had finished our beers.

We excused ourselves, explaining our mission to our new friend. That's when it happened. Bahssten picked up what looked to be an enormous forty ounce sized cup of beer and handed it to me.

"Here," she said, "You can have dis one. Deeze guys buy em for me fasta' than I can drink em!"

That was where I batted my eyes and little hearts started floating around the room. Not really, but you get the point. Starting that night, the three of us were inseparable.

After the wrestling match ended, Red and I, along with our new alcohol-loving friend, headed out to a bar. Before we hopped in the car, I stumbled upon a crushed box next to a rusty, fly infested dumpster. Perfect, there was my spot. I pulled my panties down to my knees and unleashed my yellow river of 98.5 degree beer in the parking lot. Bahssten was not used to my behavior quite yet. She thought this was incredible and snapped a picture.

Upon dive bar arrival, Red told us about a girl she had just met at work. She thought maybe she should call and see if this girl wanted to join us. Bahssten and I were so torn up at that point that we loved everyone. Of course, we agreed with this plan.

Soon, a chubby blonde with amazing cheek bones walked in. This girl reminded me of a girl I dated (Lady) a few years prior. Immediately, I developed a small girl-crush on her. She was wearing a long, black skirt and a violet shirt with three buttons on the top. I noticed a little embroidered deer on the far right corner of her chest. She said hello and we began our introductions.

Her name was Flowa', that's right, "Fla-oww-wa." I approached the bar and bought her what would later become our signature cocktail, an apple martini.

After a few drinks, our new friend looked down at her shirt. In a sudden panic she exclaimed, "Oh, my God! What is that on my shirt? Is that a deer? I hate deer! I'm deathly afraid of deer! You girls all look so hot and I look like an old lady in this skirt and now I realize there's a deer on me!"

That's when it happened, I did what any caring, slurred speech having, drunken whore would do. I reached right over and ripped off Flowa's shirt. Not completely, just enough to expose her milky white tatas and tuck what was left of the "God forsaken deer" away.

    Flowa' didn't give a shit. She laughed.

    The Fun Girls were born.

Pirates & Dragons

I remember getting the call from Robin in the late afternoon. At twenty seven years old, I was a single mom, living alone with my son in Las Vegas. That day I happened to be working my usual shift at the spa and was in the back room between appointments when I heard my phone buzzing. My caller ID said it was Redbeard.

Redbeard was my high school sweetheart. Long before my obsession with Donut, there was Redbeard. He was the first man I had ever loved. He was 6' 5", with hazel eyes, natural red hair (more of the auburn persuasion than bright ginger) and a personality no one could ever match. He was radiant, dynamic and fearless.

Redbeard and I had this special connection, the kind where we would finish each other's sentences. Just a look and we had the whole idea of what the other one was thinking.

He was also the first man to give me an orgasm. Redbeard was in my top three of the best sex I had ever had. I spent years obsessing over and on-again-off-again dating him and even aborted his baby. We called it quits for good when we were twenty two, but we managed to stay close friends.

I was happy to hear from Redbeard, he hadn't text messaged me back in days and I was wondering what was going on with him. He was supposed to have come by my place the Friday night prior but cancelled last minute because he did not have a ride. Of course, I offered to pick him up but told him that I could not drive him home because we were planning on drinking. So, I suggested that he stay the night at my place. However, he had declined, saying he had plans later on that evening he just couldn't miss.

"Hello!" I said expecting to hear his bubbly, boyish voice on the line. I did not, instead it was his sister, Robin.

"Hey, *****? It's Robin. Are you sitting down right now? Cause if not you probably should."

63

I sat down.

What the fuck did Redbeard do now? Ugh! Was he in jail? I wondered. Probably he needed money. I was always helping him out, after all, I loved the guy, but he never helped himself. He better be fucking dead!

"Redbeard is dead," Robin continued. My heart shattered.

The following week I was attending a funeral service for Redbeard when I noticed a tall, nerdy boy with acne scars acting dorky in a group of his peers. Curious, I approached him with a cigarette in my mouth and asked him for a light. He lit my cigarette then immediately continued his shenanigans as if I wasn't there.

I watched him on and off for the remainder of the afternoon. At one point, I even noticed him sitting on a bench with his furry plumber crack showing. He was wearing a black t-shirt that was obviously too short for his too tall frame and jeans. On his feet he wore a pair of vans. His chin was concealed with a skinny goatee hiding some of the scars. The top of his hair was long, the sides shaved and died purple.

I honestly cannot tell you what it was, but I had "the hots" for this dweeb! That's right, my pulse was racing! Possibly, I may even have been drooling just a little.

So, that night, I did what any lonely and grieving drunk slut would do on the eve of the funeral of her ex high school sweetheart. I drank wine alone and went on Redbeard's MyPlace "friends list" to find my geek.

It didn't me take long, Morthos. There he was, acne scarred in all his glory.

I sent him a message. He immediately responded. Turns out Morthos remembered lighting my cigarette and he lived down the street from me.

What luck? Within an hour, Morthos was knocking on my door.

I fed Morthos wine. We talked, laughed and I faked some charm. Then I took him into my room, pushed him on my bed and starting sticking my dried out red wine stained tongue down his throat while dry humping him.

Next, I tried taking off his pants. He would not let me. Morthos refused to give me his warlock. That's when it happened!

I CAME!!!

Morthos' magical powers released a "big-O" from my loins without even a wave of his magical weenie wand.

He came back the next night and unleashed upon me some of the most ravaging sex I had ever had. Morthos was definitely in my top three of the best sex ever.

Morthos lorded over my ocean. This guy could make me cum with a look. My newest obsession was born. While at work, I would think about him and get wet. I would day dream about him while driving in the car and soak my seat. We sent dirty text messages to each other consistently.

Meow!

Morthos worked a late schedule. Usually, I would leave my door unlocked and go to sleep around ten at night. He would come by after his shift at work (usually around one in the morning) and wake me up.

For hours, we would passionately make out while having some of the most amazing, firework exploding sex. Morthos was only twenty three years old. He could go two, three and even four rounds sometimes. It was the type of sex that the minute he would enter me, we would have to stop moving or we would both explode with pleasure.

We gave each other back rubs and baths, he would wash my hair in the shower. I would burn candles and play sexy mixed CD's I created for each special night. Then we would pass out, Morthos making sure to have me tight in his arms. In the morning, we would awake and do it all over again.

Only one thing was wrong. Morthos would not hang out with me in public. He would not introduce me to his friends and after a while he was coming by less and less. The more he resisted the more obsessed I became.

One night he suggested holding onto my spare key so I could lock the door at night. I thought this was a brilliant idea.

My crazy, desperate self thought this meant he was ready for the next step so I asked him to move in.

That's when it happened. Morthos never came back. I called him and confessed my undying love to him a little while later. He told that me he didn't feel the same way.

One day, when I was at work he, left the key under my door mat.

A Dream Is A Wish Your Rotting Heart Makes

The first time I re-slept with Donut was roughly six months ago. We were both intoxicated and extremely giddy. He had been teasing me all day with his rock hard cock and I was making him that way with my flirting.

Donut grabbed me by the wrist and led me into his bedroom. He put his hands on my face and pulled me to him while slipping his tongue inside my mouth. Grabbing my ass, he pressed me against IT. His cock was bigger than I remembered and it curved in just the right spot.

I wish I could give you more details of this moment but I cannot. These memories are sacred to me because I love him. Well, that and I was pretty drunk.

See, it all started a few weeks prior to this day. Donut had emailed me to tell me he had left his on-again, off-again girlfriend of the last few years for good. Recently, he had relocated back to the shitty apartment complex he lived in six years ago when we had dated the first time. He told me that he wanted to take me out somewhere nice, but that I would have to wait until he moved because he could not afford it. Donut mentioned to me that he was saving up to get an apartment that happened to be a couple blocks from where I was currently residing.

I told Donut that I didn't care if he took me somewhere nice, I just wanted to see him. Really, I did, I was curious as to how the years treated him. Now I was older and more confident, I was sure I could handle him. Plus, a little part of me wanted to make him suffer for the decade of torment he had put me through. My plan was to make him fall in love with me and then I was going to break his heart.

The evening of our first date came around. Donut and I had been text messaging consistently, all week. He was going to pick me up and take me to dinner. After, we were going bowling. I told Donut from the get-go that this date was "friends only" and not to try any funny stuff.

My Cream Puff was supposed to pick me up at seven o'clock that Thursday night. It was now past seven thirty and I had not heard from him in a few hours. I had just spent a good hour before this primping and was now, unsuccessfully, getting my kids to sleep. Disappointedly, I was starting to think Donut might be flaking on me.

Around eight o'clock, just as my kids were almost snoozing and I was about to give up, I received a text message from my dough daddy. He said he had fallen asleep and apologized. Actually, he was hopping in the shower and would be on his way shortly.

This was my first sign of what was to come but I didn't care. After all this WAS revenge and I needed a night out of the house. I was not going to sleep with him, I wasn't even getting involved with him emotionally. It was just a free dinner.

Donut eventually pulled up to my house and drove me to the Mexican restaurant. We got out of the car and that's when I saw him in the light for the first time. He was still short but he was wearing a hat that flattered his face perfectly. Fine lines we beginning to appear on his face that made him look almost distinguished. Those teeth, I always think about his beautiful teeth when he smiles. Plus, he was dressed sexy, he always had his own style and was clean. He smelled good.

DAMN IT! FUCK!

That was it! This bitch was in heat. Mentally, I was putting my paws up, sticking my tongue out and panting. I wanted to walk circles around him and stick my ass in his face like a dog.

However, I held my composure.

We sat at the bar and ordered drinks, shared some food and caught up. I can't even tell you how mushy I felt inside just being next to him. All those feelings I had over the years of longing for this very moment were flooding back to me.

After dinner, we headed to the bowling alley. Donut blasted his speakers in the car, just like I remembered, while dancing along. He still had the same great taste in music. I felt like an ant in a donut shop.

Once we arrived at the bowling alley, we both got out of the car and walked inside. That's when it happened. Donut couldn't pay.

You see, that afternoon, when his shift ended at work, Donut went out for sushi. He bought himself lunch and several rounds of drinks before going home and passing out, he had spent most of his money.

I paid.

We ordered a couple pitchers of beer, grabbed our shoes and went to our lane. The more he drank the bigger of a jerk he became. Donut noticed the girl in the lane next to us. He started staring at her, relentlessly. She was not a prize. Actually, she was short and anorexically skinny with black hair and bad skin. The skimpy skirt she wore revealed too much of her pale, twig legs. Also, she had a huge hook nose.

My puffed daddy started saying things like, "I might as well look at her because you aren't gonna' put out. I mean you are way hotter but it's not like I have a chance," and "You think that guy she is with will want to trade dates?"

This is where, if I had any self-esteem at all, I would have walked out. Alas, I was a stupid slut in love. I found this charming and I played along.

"So, when did you start going bald?" I asked him, "Have you always been this short or are you shrinking with you old age?"

Donut loved this.

I kicked his ass at bowling and we finished our pitchers then headed to a dive bar. Once there, we drank on my tab and Donut kicked my ass at pool. Then, he drove me home.

That was it. That worm had re-hooked this fish.

We made plans for that following Saturday. When the morning finally arrived I made the grueling four hour (round trip) drive to drop my daughter with her dad. I was just a half-hour away from Donut's place when I texted him my location.

He responded, saying he was at the bar with the guys, finishing his last beer and would be on his way home in a few minutes. This happened to be my one free Saturday a month and I couldn't think of anything in the world better than spending it with my charming hunk of bisexual love.

Donut was planning to BBQ for me. That's right, he was cooking me dinner.

So, I did what any love-struck, self-hating, cheap slut would do. I stopped at the store and bought a case of beer, a case of water and some chocolate for dessert.

I love chocolate.

After shopping, I stopped at a public bathroom to release my bowels and "hooker shower" in preparation. A girl never wants to poop at a man's house before marriage, that's dating rule number one.

Once my intestines were emptied and I was body-odor free, I excitedly headed out to my rotting, dream shack. I arrived a half an hour after my text message.

I parked on the side street by Donut's run down abode and called to tell him I had arrived. My maple bar didn't answer.

Next, I walked up to his stoop while looking in the driveway, no car. I knocked on his termite ridden door, no answer. Strange! I sent him another text, "Donut, I'm at your house. I will wait five minutes for you and then I'm leaving."

Ten minutes later my phone rang, it was my rainbow sprinkle!

"Why are you leaving?" he drunkenly whined, "I'm just finishing up this beer and I'll be on my way."

"Listen, Crumb Cake, you said that a half-hour ago. I'm hanging up my phone now and setting my alarm. You get ten minutes and then I'm leaving!" I warned.

Now, this is where I really should have hauled my beautiful little blonde self out of there and to any public place alone. I could have found a better man than that in ten minutes, tops! But I didn't, I love him!

I sat there for a half-hour.

When Donut finally did show up he was tossed. His car swerved up the road barely missing mine. With his radio blaring, he pulled up next to me.

"Get in," he ordered, without opening the door or helping me with the groceries. That apple fritter is so damn hot when he's demanding.

I got in, but not until I made him get out and carry the groceries. That's right, I put that bitch in check.

He drove us up to his apartment. Once inside, he opened me a beer. Then, he apologized for being late and started a "funny because it's really fucked up," awkward and wasted conversation with me.

Ahhhh, I was home!

Seven hours, one food fight and a case of beer later, Donut made love to me. Ok, he probably got me on all fours and destroyed my anus but like I said, it's a little fuzzy.
I just remember after.
The minute he expelled his cream-filled load and put his arm around me, I ran. Literally.
I grabbed my clothes, my heels and my bag and I marathon sprinted all the way back to the car. Donut came running after me, "Where are you going? Can I walk you out?" he begged.
"No!" I shouted back to him, "I gotta go!"
"Well, are you still going to the show with me next week, at least?" he desperately asked.
"No! Well, yeah or maybe. I don't know. Call me."

Eat your heart out, fairy tale princess! There he was, my cream filled, sugar sprinkled, hot dough of a prince and he was hooked.

Well, for a few weeks, anyway. That's another story.

Tiny The Turkey

It was a crisp fall day in a small Idaho town. The year was 1990. I was roughly ten years old. My dad had taken my brothers and me to his friend Larry's house for the day. Larry happened to live on a turkey farm.

Thanksgiving was quickly approaching. Larry told us that the turkeys were about to be sold off and slaughtered for the holiday. My ten year old brain did not like this. I needed to save one, I needed a plan.

So, I watched while my dad and Larry enjoyed a few beers. I waited for their cheeks to get rosy and their speech to slur slightly. Then, it was time.

"Daddy, can I have a pet turkey?" I begged.

"They are Larry's turkeys, honey. You have to ask him."

"Okay," I said turning to Larry, "Larry, (batting lashes) can I have one of your turkeys?" I asked.

Larry, being buzzed and looking for some entertainment, thought he could outsmart me, "Sure, Honey! If you can catch one, it's all yours!"

Game on.

I hopped over a fence and into the pen to look around. As I began to make my first move, I saw it.

Gimp turkey.

I rushed towards the damn thing, as fast as my ten year old legs would carry me. The mass of birds started flapping their wings and running. All, except one. It tripped over itself and wasn't even a challenge.

The handicapped are drawn to me.

Now, I don't know if it was because of the shock, all the beer or perhaps that Larry and my dad are men of their word, but I got to keep my prize.

I climbed into the back seat of my dad's car that evening proud, I had saved a life. Tiny the turkey, sat on my lap. My dad started the engine. That's when it happened, the bird shit on my lap. It was like a water balloon of smelly, hot "White Out" exploded all over me.

My dad stopped the car and I put Tiny in the trunk.

We talked my grandpa into letting me keep it at his place, in his barn. What Tiny lacked physically he made up for mentally. He would jump up and pull the chain to the barn light all night long.

> On and off.
> On and off.
> On and off.

This was quite the feat with only one good leg. Grandpa grew tired of this quickly and suggested Tiny move out before he became dinner.

Not long after, a boy from my bible class joyfully adopted Tiny. A week later, that boy's dog ate him.

Jelly Belly Shelly

It was late morning on a Sunday in July. Shelly and I walked out of the ice cream shop on Fourth Street, already wasted from our morning binge drinking.

"I don't even want this fucking ice cream! Why did you buy it for me?" Shelly asked.

Shelly was booze-a-rexic. This meant she never ate food in any form. She had a bloated beer gut attached to a tall, skinny frame.

"Because it's fucking hot! Eat the ice cream, Bitch!"

"I'm gonna throw it on the ground!" Shelly threatened.

"Put it in there," I said pointing to a public, mail box, "I dare you."

Sure as shit, that drunk bitch pulled down the latch to the door and dropped the sucker in there! I couldn't believe it.

A black woman in a sedan saw the whole thing. She rolled her window down, "Bitch, I know you didn't just throw your ice cream in the mail box! I'm gonna' pull over and whoop your skank, white ass!"

Shelly threw her arms up, "Bring it on, Bitch!"

Oh, shit!

In fear of a tooshy whoopin', I did what any evil, drunken jerk would do when her friend was about to get her face smashed in. I fled the scene of the crime. That's right, I ran like hell.

Two blocks later, I made it home. Shelly wasn't far behind.

"Why did you run? That bitch wasn't gonna' do shit. I flipped her off and she drove away."

Shelly was almost two decades older than I was but you couldn't tell by the way she dressed. She loved platforms, six inches or higher, peroxide and black eye shadow. Actually, she wore more makeup than a transvestite prostitute.

One time, Shelly spent the night at a mutual friend's house that happened to have had white pillow cases. He said when Shelly left the next morning she literally left behind a carbon copy of her face one of his pillows.

    Bammy-Tae-Faker.
    Shelly was an alcoholic. Not the kind of weekend warrior alcoholic I was, she was the real deal. This girl would wake up to a tall glass of straight, room temperature, no-name vodka and shoot it in one gulp.
    Then, she would open up my kitchen cabinets and grab glasses yelling, "I'm going to throw this on the ground and smash it!" for no reason what so ever.
    She was constantly getting us thrown out of bars and other venues. Once, she even kicked the mirrored backdrop at a dance club, shattering the entire thing.
    I liked hanging out with Shelly because she made ME look good.

    We worked together at a hair salon. Shelly would walk in sober but by her second appointment, she was shit faced and verbally abusive, bullying the poor person in her chair.
    This brought me much joy.
    "You want me to do what? I'm not going to cut your hair like that! That's fucking stupid! You would look like an idiot!" she would scream at her client.

    Eventually, Shelly got fired. Then, she died.

The Grossest Thing I Ever Did, Maybe

I'm sure tonight Brutus is throwing a big event down at the Lit Fart. Right about now he has some dumb slut sucking him off in his office. I'm okay with that because I know that no girl will ever do for Brutus the things I did. Brutus may have been the worst lay of my life time but I am certain that I am the best lay of his and I'm going to tell you why.

A few weeks into my courtship with my mullet man, I pulled my car into the parking lot of the Lit Fart.

I clicked my little muscular skank legs inside and took a seat at the bar. The bartender recognized me and served me my regular piss water in a bottle aka Bob Light.

There was a Beat-alls Tribute band playing that night. They were wearing horrible wigs and the most absurd 1960's themed costumes I had ever seen.

They were ridiculous in all ways. I hate the Beat-alls.

Brutus said hello and then wandered off to do his usual OCPD shit. I sat there, drank my urine juice and did my best not to "Boo!" between songs.

An hour or so later Brutus whisked me off onto our official first date.

He led me to a tiny, red, go-cart of a car, really. Brutus told me it was a rental. He liked it though, because of the "great gas mileage." I'm still not sure if he was joking.

We headed out to downtown for dinner.

"I want to be straight with you," Brutus began, "I'm really busy right now with my bar. It dominates my whole life. I just don't have a lot of time for a relationship. If this were ten years ago and I met a cool, hot blonde I'd say to myself, 'Let's do this!' However, right now, I just don't have the time."

"Look, Brutus," I said, "I have two young kids and a career. I don't have a lot of free time either. I'm just looking for someone I can hang out with, consistently, roughly once a week. Right now, I cannot take on anything more than that. Though, I'm not going to stick around for a fling, I don't want to get involved just to be told several months down the line nothing will ever come of this because I have young children."

Donut did that.

"Some men let their egos get the best of them," he said.

Brutus is smart.

"I'm open to the possibility of something more down the line. Who's to say a few years from now my work load won't be different. I don't know what will happen in the future, I can only speak for right now. Are we clear on this?"
"We are on the same page," I agreed.
Brutus put his sexy hand on my leg. This got me wet.
After parking the car, we walked into the restaurant. Brutus took the initiative to order for me. I love that in a man. Especially when he is educated enough to order well and has good taste, Brutus was both. Then, he pulled me toward him and put my hand on his dick. It was hard. I rubbed it.
The server came with our Sangria. Brutus encouraged me to caress him, more. He loved PDA and made sure that our waiter saw what I was doing under the table. My chunk-o-wrestler liked to show me off.
"You do that well. Do you like to rub my cock?" Brutus asked me.
"Of course!" I chirped.
"Tell me you like to rub it then."
I giggled. Brutus is such a flirt!
Next, Brutus decided to tell me a story, "You, rubbing my cock like that, reminds me of the Asian girl at the massage parlor."
"You know, I work for a spa, right?" I asked Brutus, "Not that kind of a spa, though."
"Oh, they give great hand jobs at your kind of spas, too. I was in a five star hotel when I had a woman rub me down really good. It was taking me a long time to finish. She reached her face down near my cock to get some more oil and I accidentally released myself all over her face and uniform. I made sure to give her a good tip. Imagine walking around all

day with a strangers load on your clothes and a blood shot eye."

I laughed, a little. Brutus' stories are not as good as mine.

"I like to tell that story to women just to see their reactions. To see if they will freak out," he added.

I'm sure my reaction was disappointing to Brutus. We had something in common. Both of us liked it better when the other wasn't talking. Uh huh, we had what you could call, "a clash of narcissism."

Finally, Brutus had all the teasing he could take.

"Let's get back to the bar!" he suggested with a smug smile. Brutus was hot.

Once inside the closed establishment, he turned on a dull light. Then, he sat on a couch and unbuttoned his pants.

"Come here," he ordered.

I complied.

He started stroking his Jew stick. Once he was erect, he grabbed my head and pulled me towards him. I started sucking on his salty spud sacs. Gently, I put my finger in his un-groomed anus.

After a few minutes, Brutus told me to get up. He pulled down my panties, lifted up my skirt and bent me over the arm of the couch. I could hear him sucking the saliva from his tongue before he spit it onto my dirty asshole.

It was lubed up good enough for Brutus.

Brutus Holo-accosted me. He was marching through Germ-many. I was getting close.

"You better get ready to finish up. I'm about to cum and when I do you are gonna' be kicked out, Bub," I warned.

I'm not sure Brutus understood me, because before I could have any of my own pleasure, he pulled out his partisan and resumed his old place on the couch. The sensation to orgasm was gone. He had destroyed my concentration camp.

Brutus wanted me to go down on him. That's right! He wanted me to put his dick in my mouth after it had just left my gas chamber.

So, I did what any cheap slut after half a pitcher of Sangria would do, I took it like a pro, in my mouth.

First, I could smell it. Then, I could taste it. Yup, I was eating my own shit. I was shit faced, literally.

It was horrible and I wanted to die. I couldn't even finish him off.

I did do one last thing though, I kissed him. He didn't even mind.

A few days after this particular date, I was texting with Brutus:

Me: I want to do some nasty things to you, you hot Stud!
Brutus: Like what?
Me: Definitely NOT what I did to you the other night! I will never do that again, unless it was your birthday or Christmas. That was disgusting.
Brutus: Why?
Me: That was the grossest thing I have ever done. I tasted shit for days. Did you ever clean that couch BTW?
Brutus: What? No, you didn't. No, I haven't cleaned it yet.
Me: Oh, God!
Brutus: Always ATM (ass to mouth).

Baby Road Kill

I was attending cosmetology school in California, I was eighteen years old. Redbeard and I were trying to have a long distance relationship. If by long distance, I mean Redbeard was still screwing dirty skanks in Las Vegas while sending me love letters and calling me nightly.

The holidays were approaching, I had two weeks of school vacation coming up and I couldn't think of anything better in the world than to spend it with my tall, long haired, pirate captain. So, I made plans to drive down to Las Vegas and see him.

I remember working my regular six hour shift at my shitty, retail job the night before, I have not had a longer shift at any job since, ever. Oh, my God, I was so excited.

The night before I barely got any sleep. By nine o'clock that morning, I hit the road. That afternoon, I arrived in town with a giant smile on my face and a puddle in my panties. Just as I pulling down Redbeard's street, I saw it.

I slammed on my breaks.

There, in the middle of the lane, was a giant, black Labrador. Other than panting, the dog was not moving. I honked my horn, it still did not budge.

That's when I realized it. The dog had been hit by a car.

After I opened the door, I pulled myself out of my vehicle and walked towards the dog. All the while, I debated on what to do, it was huge. Obviously, I could not lift it but I could not leave it there to die, either (I used to like dogs, you know, before I had children).

I needed a plan.

I was just a few yards from Redbeard's apartment. So, I got back in the car and hauled ass to Redbeard's door. I ran to the stoop and knocked. He answered with a giant grin and his arms open, waiting to pull me to him.

I gave him a halfhearted hug and said, "Come with me! Get in the car I need your help!"

Redbeard was reluctant.

"Why?" he asked, "That wasn't much of a hug!"

"Because, there is a dog on the road that was hit by a car. We need to take him to a vet, I can't lift him on my own."

Redbeard stood there silently, "No," he finally said.

"What?" I asked in shock, "You can't say no!"

"Listen, I walk that way to work every day. If I help you get the dog and it doesn't live, then I'll have to think about this every day when I walk by," Redbeard explained.

"What?" was he serious? "Get in the fucking car, now!"

Redbeard got in the car. When we arrived near the dog, we saw that someone had already moved it to the sidewalk. A man had stopped while I was gone and was trying to help it.

We kept on driving. I thought of Redbeard a bit differently after that.

Later in the evening, Redbeard made sweet love to me. He kissed me like a hunk in a romance novel would, making my body quiver and shake in a moment of passion that pretty much was his standard.

When it was all over, we cuddled and talked about our future together. Then, Redbeard decided to confess a secret to me. In his arms, listening to music, while hopelessly in love with my landlocked sea lord, Redbeard confessed to me that his female roommate had sucked him off just a few days prior.

Yup. She had sucked him off.

I should have gone home that night, or the following morning. Instead, I stayed and tortured myself. When Redbeard went to work, I did something that I have never done before nor will ever do again in my life, I snooped through his belongings. In his drawer, I found dirty panties and love letters from other girls.

This hurt and it pissed me off. Of course, Redbeard and I had never actually had a talk about monogamy. He reminded me of this, I eventually forgave him.

A month had passed since my trip. I was accelerating in school. As a matter of fact, I was out on the salon school floor,

I had my own station and I was taking real clients. It seemed that I had found my calling, I was a natural.

One afternoon, halfway through a haircut, I felt something trickle down my leg.

That was strange! My period wasn't due yet. Or was it? Actually, yeah it was. Wait, when was my last period? Before Christmas. I was doing the calculations in my head, wondering if I should stop mid-way through my service and go to the bathroom, when it happened. Before I could even put down my comb, a river was set loose. I looked down to see my feet were standing in the middle of a puddle.

A puddle of blood.

Right there in school, halfway through a haircut with a client in my chair I was having a miscarriage. I didn't even know I was pregnant.

Thank God, I was wearing all black. I threw a towel down on the floor, ran to the bathroom and cleaned myself up the best I could.

Then, do you know what I did? I went back and I finished that damn haircut.

The bleeding continued for eight days. I was young and stupid, I didn't know what was going on until I finally went to the doctor on the eighth day. He confirmed my suspicion.

That night I called Redbeard and explained to him what happened. He was sad for me but there was nothing he could do.

This was not the last time Redbeard knocked me up, but that's another story.

Donuts Are A Girl's Best Friend

The second-to-last time I saw Donut was roughly four months ago. We had been arguing a lot through text messages. I was pushing for more of a commitment from Donut and he was pushing for less. Eventually, I told him that seeing him once a week wasn't working for me and that I wanted to see him twice a week. Also, we needed to include our kids. There was no way in hell he would budge on the kid issue.

Donut sent me a text, "You are the funnest girl ever and a goddess, but I just can't do it. Besides, once a week keeps you perfect!"

What did this mean?

As had become our usual routine, we compromised. We would still see each other just once a week but with sleepovers, occasional dinners and he was to treat me like I was his girlfriend. Just, NO KIDS.

The following Thursday night, in the skankiest little dress I could dig out of my closet and the red, slutty stilettos I bought specifically to wear for him, I made my fifteen minute drive to Donut's love shack.

Tonight was a special night. Donut had purchased bridal lingerie for me to wear and all week had been calling me by my new sex name, "Mrs. Donut." He even requested that I wear my old wedding and engagement rings.

I remember walking alone into his room. He had the outfit waiting on the bed for me.

Excitedly, I slipped on the corset top and laced it up, pulled on a white garter belt and attached a pair of translucent white thigh highs. I peeked out the bedroom door and into the living room to see my man pastry on his couch, giving me a look of anticipation. That's right, Donut wanted me, bad!

Fuck! He was so hot sitting there looking like a rapist.

"Should I wear my hair up or down?" I shouted.

"Up!" he responded breathlessly.

I slipped my hair into a pony tail and then secured the veil.

Donut watched me like a hawk watches a mouse as I left his bedroom and approached his lap. I straddled him for a second, kissed the back of his neck and breathed hotly into his ear.

Then, I got up and headed confidently towards his front door. I slipped on my heels and almost fell, we both laughed.

Practically naked, I stepped outside. Sitting on his porch, I teased him while smoking a cigarette. Halfway through Donut had had enough of my game. He grabbed my hand and pulled me to his bedroom.

That night Donut unleashed upon me some of the most unconventional, filthy sex I've ever had. Actually, that's a lie. He unleashed upon me that night: THE FILTHIEST, MOST UNCONVENTIONAL SEX I HAD EVER HAD and probably will ever have.

I'd love to give you more details, but like I said before, these experiences are precious to me. They are mine because I love him. Plus, I was a little drunk.

I only saw him once after that.

Talk About Being Stuck

I was twelve years old and spending the entire summer grounded in my room when it happened. Amid what I thought would be just another extremely boring afternoon my mom flung open my bedroom door.

"Do you have any super glue?" she asked me, her face radiating in laughter.

"In the drawer," I lazily pointed out. I was feeling alone and defeated and was in no mood for her games.

"Get it for me! Hurry!" she ordered.

Sluggishly, I rolled my fat ass off the bed and opened the drawer. I handed her the glue.

"Stay right here," she said, "I'm about to get your father back. It's going to be really funny."

With that, she walked out of my room carrying the glue. She had her hand over her mouth trying to contain her laughter.

A few minutes went by and then she came to the door of my bedroom and silently signaled me out with a wave of her hand. I reluctantly followed her into the living room.

My dad was asleep on the couch with his mouth wide open, drooling. I watched my mom slowly climb on top of him until she was straddling his lap. Then, she kissed his neck and pressed her breasts into his face

"Honey," she whispered seductively, "Wake up baby, I have a surprise for you."

My dad started to wake up. What happened next scared the shit out of me. He screamed, not a normal scream, this was the scream of someone dying. I will never forget the sound that came bellowing out of his half asleep, still a bit drunk, startled mouth.

"You fucking bitch!" he yelled as he tried to get up but moving was just making it worse. My dad grabbed his junk, fell to the floor and into the fetal position.

I didn't know it at the time, but my mom had used my superglue to attach my dad's penis to his leg. After she waited a few minutes for the glue to dry, she called me out to witness the torture. That's when she hopped on him in an attempt to excite him. Her attempt obviously worked causing my daddy's baby maker to be torn to shreds.

    I don't really want to discuss my dad's private part anymore but I'm sure you get the drift.

    It was the longest summer of my life.

Fungually Yours

While attending cosmetology school in California and just after having recently broken it off with Redbeard, I was young, hot, single and ready to mingle. My friend Sofia decided to set me up on a blind date with her friend Hanson at a local burger joint.

I left school on my lunch break and was greeted on the outside patio by Sofia and a boy a year and a half younger than I was.

That's right, at the ripe old age of 18, I was a cougar. Or perhaps a child predator, depends on how you look at it.

"This is Hanson," Sofia introduced.

I peered into Hanson's giant green eyes for the first time. He was tall, a little over six feet and really slender. Yet, he had a ghetto booty. His nose was slightly hooked and his chin a little weak, much like my own. As a matter of fact people sometimes would mistake us for siblings. We liked this, actually, we encouraged it. Then, we would make out in front of said people. This disgusted them very much.

Hanson and I both had the same raw sense of humor. We liked to do things that made most people want to vomit.

I remember one romantic evening in Hanson's spider infested, converted garage of a room. He lit a sexy, scented candle and then told me that just the night before he had stuck that very same lighter up his ass. I told Hanson he was full of shit and to prove it. Never one to back down from a dare, he pulled his green velvet, tiger striped pants down to his knees. Using his hands, he spread his bulbous butt cheeks and stuck that sucker right up his butt hole. Well, the tip anyway. Hanson was a pussy, he failed this dare.

Hanson also had a huge dick. He liked to "do" odd things with it such as my "knee pit." I have no idea where he came up with this idea or term but I finally let him do it just to get him to shut the hell up about it.

One day, a few weeks into our blossoming relationship, Hanson received what appeared to be a spider bite on his foot. This was a slight annoyance at first but as the days went by his "bite" was not healing, it was actually getting worse.

I took Hanson with me to a graduation dinner for a fellow cosmetology student one evening after the bite. Hanson was limping. So, I told him to quit being a wuss, he was embarrassing me. After all, I couldn't have my friends thinking I was dating a gimp.

Alas, the days came and went, the limping got worse and Hanson still ignored his spider bite.

I was driving home from work one afternoon when it happened. There was Hanson, rolling down the street, wearing those stupid, neon green, tiger print pants in a wheel chair.

Laughing so hard, I almost crashed. I wanted to stop for him, I really did, but I could not risk having anyone see me pick up that hot mess.

So, I did what any non-caring, selfish bitch of a girlfriend would do. I drove by honking and yelled, "Retard" out the window while flipping him off.

The next day Hanson finally saw a doctor. It turned out he didn't have a spider bite after all. Hanson had a neglected case of athlete's foot. Luckily, I myself never had to witness his disease first hand. This was a good thing because apparently the smell was so horrendous that when he finally took his sock off in the doctor's office that day, the poor, pregnant doctor literally jumped in shock before grabbing the nearest trash can to hurl in.

I saw Hanson a couple years ago when his band played in Las Vegas and you know what? He was wearing those stupid pants!

Pretty Kitty

The last year of my marriage was the hardest. My ex husband, Beans, had gone out on disability due to an injury and I picked up my third job to make ends meet. This third job was my newest adventure in the cosmetology world, instructing. After attaining my instructor's license, I was given my very own class.

In the evenings, I taught freshman room. That meant I had the students from their very beginnings into the magical land of beauty. The moment a student touched a head of hair for the first time, I could see if they were going to be in the right field of work or not.

Each new class started the same way, with a trip to the shampoo bowl. I would have a volunteer sit down, place a towel around their neck and demonstrate the basic art of shampooing. First, I would turn on the water, grab onto the hose and place the nozzle on the volunteer's head.

"Okay, class," I would say, "This is the water hose. Shampoo and conditioner will make your hands very slippery. At some point in your life, you will accidentally let go of the hose. When this happens do not try to catch the hose, simply turn the off the water."

After a quick demonstration, I let each student take turns washing each other's hair. At some point in the process, it would happen. A student would let go of the hose. The water pressure forced the hose into the air while spewing out liquid like a fire hydrant. The hose resembled a cobra, dancing in the air, soaking the room and everyone in its path. The student, dumb with shock, would try with all her/his might to catch the hose. This is when I would remind his/her stupid ass to, "Simply turn the water off."

Towards the end of freshman room students were taught the basics of waxing. To prepare for this module I went to the beauty supply and bought myself wax, a melting pot, tongue suppressors, baby powder and cloth strips. Everything needed for a successful hair removal job. Then I found a model, Beans!

After a long happy hour and several margaritas, I decided to flex my rusty waxing muscles. Even though I had been the industry for over a decade, my focus had not been on waxing. Although I knew the basics, I lacked the practice. Therefore, I did what any drunken, inexperienced, husband-hating fat ass would do. I made Beans cry, that's right.

First, I put a big sheet down on the bed. I heated up my little wax pot to max temperature. Beans laid face up on the sheet as instructed while I sprinkled baby powder all over his beastly chest.

Oh wait, no I didn't! I forgot that important step.

Instead, I picked up a tongue suppressor and started smearing hot wax all over the Bean's sweaty chest rug. He screamed out in pain. I told him to suck it up and to quit being a pussy.

I am sure I had the wax setting up too high because his skin looked like it was starting to blister. Gleefully, I smiled to myself. Once the wax fully covered his skin, I laid the strips on top and rubbed them down smoothly with the palms of my hands. Then, I prepped his skin by stretching it firmly before quickly peeling off the strips.

No, wait, I forget that step too!

I just pulled the strips away while giggling, ripping off chunks of skin along with the hair. Beans began bleeding. Not wanting me to think he was a wimp he stayed there and let me continue my torture. I was enjoying this very much so. After about a half-hour, blistered and bloody, Beans had finally had enough.

As I ripped that last strip of wax off, he jumped from the bed and screamed at me, "That's e-fucking-nuff!"

He ran down the stairs and hid in the backyard.

I wasn't done yet, I still had both of his furry legs to do. Alas, there was no way he was going to let me touch him again with any wax. We'd had a similar experience years prior with a manicure and cuticle nippers after a few too many martinis. Beans was not a quick study.

Heh heh heh.

I really didn't do it entirely on purpose, though I did enjoy inflicting the torture. I'm just a really bad waxer.

Still, I had a class to teach.

So, I did what any smart and caring educator would do in my position. I asked the aesthetics instructor if I could bring my class to her room for a demonstration near the end of the module. Luckily for all parties concerned, Ms. Veronica agreed.

Making sure to warn my students in advance about this change, they asked me what we would he waxing. I told them the usual, arm pits, legs and maybe eyebrows or lips.

A few weeks later, I took my class into the aesthetician classroom. Ms. Veronica had a bed set up in the middle of the room with chairs all around it. She instructed my students to take the seats closest to the bed.

They did, sitting down one by one. I took a standing position behind them.

One of Ms. Veronica's students volunteered to be the waxing model. Excitedly, the aesthetic student made her way to the front of the class and approached the bed. That's when it happened.

The student dropped her pants and her underwear exposing her furbie. She climbed up onto the table and without any hesitation at all, spread her legs wide open.

My students gasped, little Maria turned red and put her hands over her eyes. One student even turned to me pleading, "Miss *****?"

So, I did what any stunned and confused, curious, vagina-entranced person would do, I "shushed" her.

You see, of all my years in the field I myself had never seen a Brazilian wax performed. I figured, hey, at least these students would have a better education than most of their peers. Plus, I was new at all this and not sure what I was supposed to teach. Ms. Veronica had been teaching for over twenty years, she wouldn't steer me wrong. Would she?

Ms. Veronica was Russian. She still had the accent after decades of living in the United States. Her voice was stern and loud.

"Okay class!" she started, "Let me tell you deb first thing about deb vagina. Deb vagina is STUPID! When I touch deb vagina it gets wet. It tinks I'm a man! First we must powda' deb vagina to dry it out. Deb wax will not stick to any skin dat tis moist!"

Ms. Veronica then grabbed a bottle of baby powder and sprinkled it onto her student's fuzzy peach.

"Okay class! Next we get deb wax and test it to make sure it's not too hot."

She did this with large deft gestures, showing the group, "Now, we take deb wax and smooth it onto deb skin. First, let me pull deb skin tightly. Look here at deb fold of deb vagina."

Ms. Veronica now pulled on the lip of her student's vagina exposing the soft pink tissue inside, "Dis skin is very thin. Make sure you do not get wax in dis tender area or you will make her bleed."

Ms. Veronica reached for her wax, and then suddenly, she paused, "Ohhhhh! Look at dat! I just pulled deb vagina and already it got excited! See, it's all wet. Stupid vagina! It tinks' im a man! MORE POWDA'!"

Continuing her demonstration, Ms. Veroica applied the wax, then grabbed the strip and pulled it off. Along with the strip came the wax and a good section of pubic hair. This was soft wax, a little too soft I suppose because that is when it happened.

A chunk of pubic encrusted wax came off the strip and was flung weightlessly into the air.

It landed on Maria's shirt. Maria was horrified.

"Ms. Veronica! Some wax just landed on me! Can you get it off?" Maria begged.

"You bay quiet, Maria. You are interrupting class! I will get it for you after deb demonstration."

In desperation, Maria looked back at me. I gave her a stern look that advised she had better listen to Ms. Veronica.

The instruction lasted another hour, Maria continuously glancing down at her shirt. Poor Maria, she sat there holding back her gag reflex for the remainder of the class.

Finally, it was break time. Maria waited patiently for Ms. Veronica to scrape her shirt clean but instead, Ms. Veronica disappeared. She was in the teacher's lounge eating her dinner.

I hadn't realized this was happening because I had stepped out for a cigarette break myself. When I noticed Maria was still "pubic-ridden" I went on a hunt for Ms. Veronica. After finding Ms. Veronica in the lunch room, she told me that she would remove the wax after break and she kept her promise. After all, what was twenty more minutes at this point?

I was disgusted for Maria but I was also secretly laughing on the inside.

After the break ended, the students met back in classroom and Maria was scraped clean. It was now time for the practical portion of the instruction and groups were formed. Two of my students were each matched up with one of Ms. Veronica's students and put into private waxing rooms to try out what they just learned on each other. This was when I bailed.

As my poor students were searching for me to help them, I realized that I really knew nothing about this subject and didn't want to hurt their learning process. Plus, I had had my fill of pussy for the day. I told them to go to Ms. Veronica for help as I hid outside, smoked cigarettes and texted the details to Beans for the last two hours of school.

The final weeks of that module were hell. My class had lost respect for me, they no longer took instruction and most of their grades suffered because of it. I knew then that teaching was not my calling.

Date-a-Douche.Com

I was freed from the marriage of Beans in the spring of 2011. At thirty years old and a size fourteen, I looked and felt like shit. That's when I started walking.

Six months and sixty pounds later I decided it was time to start dating. After transforming myself into a major babe, I had reestablished my confidence. I even had an appointment for an audition to pose nude in a magazine a few weeks away.

So, I did what any single, newly slender, desperate, money hungry bimbo would do. That's right, I joined a dating site. Once registered, I spent many hours creating the perfect profile. I uploaded several slutty pictures of myself and began my man hunt. Within 24 hours, I had over 150 responses.

Let me give you a quick rundown of the online dating world in case you are considering trying it yourself. The majority of the men on the site have been on there for years waiting for you. They have already had sex with or tried to have sex with every other woman who has a profile over a week old. Literally, they have been sitting in front of their computers just waiting for you to join. You are now considered "fresh meat." Not only this but I want you to know, men do not read your profile. Nor have they any clue what you are really looking for. Much like a small child, they only look at the pictures.

Being overwhelmed by all the attention, I decided to start at email number one. It was generic enough. I looked at his profile, tattoos. Okay, that's my type. Income over $150,000 a year, check. He said he was a movie director of sorts. We had dining in common. The site said we were a match. He was a bit chubby but as a former fat ass myself, who was I to judge? I'm not shallow. So, I wrote Butterball back.

Butterball's emails were funny and witty, this guy had attitude! After a few days of emailing, I gave him my phone number and we started texting.

Three solid days of conversation later, Butterball sent me a picture. I opened it up to discover that it was taken at his high school prom. Butterball was dressed up like a pimp. I'm serious, he had on a leopard print tux, a top hat and was carrying a cane. Then, I noticed his date, a stick-thin brunette whose head looked to be photo enhanced onto her body. I asked Butterball if his date was a real person. He said she was real, alright. In fact, she was a real hooker.

A week after our initial online match was made, Butterball and I met for lunch at a restaurant near my house. It was New Year's Day. What better way to start off the new year than by a first date? I didn't know it at the time but Butterball had just traveled over 70 miles to see me, even though I had specifically requested in my profile, that my dates live within a 30 mile radius. I didn't know it at the time that men couldn't read.

Once I pulled up to the restaurant, I sent Butterball a text message verifying my arrival. He told me to meet him at the bar. After getting out of the car, I checked my makeup, adjusted my bra and made sure all my loose stomach skin was tucked into my jeans. "Here goes nothing," I thought to myself as I clanked up the steps in my six inch heels entering the restaurant.

That's when I saw him for the first time. His bulbous arm waved to me. Oh, shit. What had I done?

Confidently, I walked right over to Butterball. He was watching me approach with a twinkle in his eye. I looked him up and down. Then, while looking him directly in his fat face, I shook my head.

"Nah, sorry," I said as I had begun to walk away. After a few steps, I stopped, turned around and started laughing so hard I thought I would piss myself. I was just messing with him.

First, Butterball was angry, then he was confused, this was followed by relief. I had never seen so many emotions cross a person's face in so little time, in all of my life.

Butterball bought me a peach cider and he handed it to me just as we were following the waitress out to the patio to be seated. We sat down and he complimented my "beautiful eyes" before telling me the story of how he had to hire a hooker to take his loser ass to prom. I must admit I liked the confession and I even felt a little sorry for my hunk-o-meat. He deserved some free pussy, just not on that date. I never put out until at least the third.

I sat across from Butterball, listening to him ramble on about himself for hours. As he talked, I could smell the distant stench of rotting teeth drifting towards me. Butterball reminded me of a Thanksgiving turkey. He was fairly tall and almost exactly as round. Not fat per se, he was just really swollen. You know that moment when you remove your holiday table centerpiece from the oven, the skin is golden brown and the juices are right underneath waiting for the first press of the knife to come exploding out. That's what Butterball looked like. Even the way the skin of a turkey has little bumps all over it from where the feathers were plucked out, Butterball had those too. Only his were in the form of skin tags. Even the creases of his eyes had skin tags dangling from them. His face was so swollen all that remained of his eyes were little slits. They looked like coin slots. I literally sat there wondering what would happen if I attempted to insert a quarter into one of them as he rambled on. I noticed that the effort it took Butterball to make even the smallest movement caused him to sweat. Also, he was a Jew.

Yet, I went on a second date with Butterball. My chunky meat cake, being a hot shot movie director, worked "on set." He was very busy and his time was limited. Still, he continued to text me throughout the day. One fateful Friday, he had his assistant book him a room at a hotel in my neighborhood. Butterball explained it was so he could take me out and not have to worry about making the long, 70 mile drive home after our date.

"Yah, right! Don't even think about it, Bub, I'm not stupid. You are not getting ANY from me tonight. I don't put out until at least the third date," I texted him.

Butterball just laughed at me and told me to meet him at the hotel at six o'clock. He gave me his room number.

I replied, "I'm not meeting you in a hotel room. You might rape and murder me."

"Please, everyone knows me, besides there will be no raping needed!"

One of the things I really admired about Butterball was his ego. He definitely had a warped sense of self and despite his monstrous looks, lived in the land of self-delusion.

Seriously, he thought he was famous and probably good looking, too. I had already done a background check on him, he wasn't a convicted killer, but he wasn't famous either.

Despite my better judgment, I met Butterball in his hotel room. After knocking on the door, he greeted me with a glass of pinot grigio, my favorite. Butterball had class. I excitedly took the wine and sat on the sofa. He took his own glass and laid on the bed while turning on the TV.

After a few minutes, he said to me, "You can sit on the bed, too, you know. I won't bite."

I slowly got up and joined him, sluggishly claiming a far-off corner. Butterball had become transfixed in his program of celebrity news. I, being a woman, love that shit and became transfixed on the celebrity gossip, too.

As I sat there, silently watching, I become disturbed by a disruptive noise. It started off light but was quickly becoming more daunting, it was getter louder and heavier.

"What the fuck is that?" I wondered, looking around the room.

That's when I discovered it. The sound was coming from Butterball, he was wheezing. Politely, I tried my best to ignore it.

After roughly an hour of mindless television, three hand smacks to Butterball (he kept trying to touch my legs) and two bottles of wine later, I reminded him we still had not eaten. Lazily, he hefted his dying lungs off the bed and into the shower.

That's when I noticed it. Butterball had painted his toe nails.

He spent another hour getting ready. By the time we were heading out to eat, I was already pretty drunk. We walked down the main city street and into the restaurant. There we ate and ordered two more bottles of wine. Between courses, we took cigarette breaks. Butterball talked about the shows he was directing, all the Hollywood stars he was friends with and the $1000 pairs of shoes he had purchased for his ex girlfriend. He told me he loved to lavish gifts on women and that he was going to fly me out first class to see him on set in Colorado when his movie was produced. I'd probably be sitting next to a celebrity or two of course.

After dinner, we walked back to the hotel. Well, neither of us really walked. I stumbled and he rolled. That is where my memory ends.

Four o'clock in the morning, I woke up naked in the hotel room. Uh oh! What had I done? I was pretty sure I knew the answer. Quickly, I removed myself from the beast's bed, threw on my clothes and high tailed it out of there before IT awoke.

As I was walking through the lobby, I looked at my phone. There was a voice mail from my grandma. She had been watching my children, "*****, where are you? It's one o'clock in the morning. I was wondering where you are. Are you out drinking? You better not be drinking somewhere! You are an alcoholic! Get your ass home, you drunk!"

I am a thirty two year old baby.

Quickly, I ran to my car and hopped in attempting to leave the lot. However, the gate was closed and I was trapped. When I received my keys back after dinner, the valet hadn't mentioned that they would be closing the area for the night.

With my wrinkled clothes, smudged off eyebrows, JBF (just been fucked) hair and smelling like a mix between ogre semen and booze, I went on a security guard hunt. After twenty minutes, I finally found one. Luckily, he was able to open the gate to the lot without asking too many questions. Rushing, I got into my car and headed towards the freeway. I made a wrong turn ending up on a bridge and was unable to turn back around. The bridge led me to an island.

Two hours later, as the sun was coming up, I finally made it home.

Despite putting out on the second date, Butterball continued texting me, just not as frequently. We had a few more dates, only now I was driving out to his place.

Butterball never did buy me any shoes. He never introduced me to any celebrities, either. Actually, Butterball even stopped buying me dinner.

One morning, after a boring, four hour TV session aka date the night before, Butterball woke up with his menorah lit. He was ready for action. Despite his foul looks and putrid breath, I was still able to squeeze out some baby-Os from our sex sessions.

Butterball was not equipped with a lot. Actually, his penis reminded me of the little plug that pops out of a turkey when it's cooked. I don't think Butterball had ever hit the right internal temperature because his little plug never popped out all the way.

He had me bent over the bed and was gyrating his little Jewish candle in and out of me while wheezing and making his usual puddle of sweat on the pillow, when it happened. His ugly, little dog opened the slightly cracked bedroom door to expose his roommate on the other side with a video camera, jacking off.

Butterball pretended to be shocked, "What the hell is wrong with you, man?" he yelled at his roommate.

I scrambled off the bed, put on my clothes and left.

Anyway, I guess if this whole writing thing doesn't work out, there's that.

Donut's Sequined Slut

After I slept with Donut that night of the BBQ, everything changed. I knew I was in for it. Of course, I would go to that concert with him. Therefore, I did what any love sick, game playing, crack whore would do.

I tugged on a pair of skin tight, black sequined pants, a ripped rocker tee and a pair of six inch heels. I towered over Donut in my stilettos but he didn't mind. He loves high heels and he liked the pants too. Donut even told me that my ass looked sexy in them.

On my way to Donut's ghetto shack, I received a text message from him. He asked me if he drove us to the show, would I drive us back. I responded by saying that I thought it should be the other way around.

"You drink before the show. I'll drink during. The beer there is too expensive and I'm not buying you shit."

"Is that so? We can discuss it when I get there," I threatened.

Such a charmer, that maple bar!

By the time I arrived, Donut was already a few beers in. He pulled out a piece of paper and handed it to me. It was his STI test.

"Look," Donut said, "I don't have AIDS."

Donut paused, he blinked. Then, with his eyes to the floor he continued, "I was thinking, if I did have AIDS, you would probably have AIDS, too. Then we would have to get married because we could only fuck each other.......or I guess we could fuck other people with AIDS."

I looked at him like he was crazy, "What the hell is wrong with you?" I asked. Then I giggled. Donut is such a romantic! Here he was discussing marriage with me again.

I drank a beer with him before we headed to the show.

Once inside I was getting my usual male attention. Donut did not like this, he was insecure. I bought myself a beer.

We sat down on a picnic bench and talked. I talked, Donut actually listened. He looked me in the eyes, he was interested and it was real, God damn it!

We finished our beers and then headed up to our seats. They were probably in the worst section I had ever been in but I didn't care. I didn't even like the band, I just lied to get the date with him.

It was a chilly night. Donut gave me his gloves. That's right, I was wearing his gloves. I know what you are thinking, I sound more like an obsessed teenager than a thirty two year old mother of two, but that's how Donut always made me feel.

After a bit, we ran out of beer. We walked to the closest vendor together. Amazingly, Donut paid for my beer!

Uh huh, just after he leaned into the bartender and told him I was a cheap slut.

A cheap slut....

We ended up leaving the show early. On the way out Donut had linked arms with me because of the steep walk back to the car. A man passed by us and said to my cream puff, "I guess dreams really do come true!"

The man then licked his lips, he was lusting over me. Donut did that weird, full body blush thing.

We went back to his place and had some of the most amazing sex ever. Donut's cream filling exploded, I convulsed. Then we woke up and did it again in the morning. I'd like to give you more details, but I cannot.

Because I love him. Also, I was pretty drunk.

Now, I still know what you are thinking, but you are wrong. A few days after that, I told Donut I might be hanging out, if by hanging out I mean having a three way, with some other guys and Donut flipped out. He was really jealous and he even accused me of looking at another guy at the concert.

For that brief moment in time, Donut totally loved me.

Cocaine: On A Cellular Level

One bright, very hung over, Sunday morning, I awoke. After caking on some foundation and a bottle of hairspray, I packed a beach bag. I also packed my "make-up kit."

This was not any ordinary kit, this particular kit was my cocaine kit. It was a shiny red make up bag that my grandmother had given to me. Inside I had what appeared to be a lip pencil. Really, it was a hollow lip liner tube that I used for snorting things. Also inside, a lovely, saliva streaked makeup mirror (I always had to lick it clean), one library card and a little, white shimmer powder, screw top, eye shadow container. I thought I was really clever. Luckily I never got caught.

Red was not the only ginger in my life back then. There was another, her name was Orange.

My little carrot stick picked me up that day and we headed down the coastal highway, making a brief pit stop at our local beauty supply for some eye shadow. We filled my container and headed to the beach. Once to the beach we grabbed our bags and headed out onto the sand. We set up camp with a huge blanket and lathered on the tanning oil. Well, I lathered on the oil. Orange, being a ginger, probably put on SPF 12,000.

We took turns passing our clever little kit back and forth. Worried about tan lines as we sunbathed, we removed our tops, lying face down on the sand. We were pretty high so, we decided to take topless pictures of each other. Okay, probably I was making Orange take topless pictures of me.

Not long after, Orange noticed two gay men playing soccer on the beach just a few yards away. Orange, being an avid soccer player and flying high on diamond dust, asked if she could join the game. The three of them kicked the ball around for a while. Feeling guilty, or possibly worried that I was "putting on the rest of the makeup," Orange wandered over to the blanket I was laying on and asked me to join the game.

At this point in my life I was fat and lazy. Unless it had to do with me bouncing up and down on a stranger or doing a strip tease across a major city block, I wasn't moving.

Instead, Strawberry Snortcake and her new friends took a break and sat on our blanket with me. I showed off my new camera phone. Our new friends asked if I wouldn't mind taking a few pictures of the two of them together on the beach. Ahhh, how romantic, of course, I wouldn't. As I sent the photos to one of their email addresses (he hadn't yet gotten a picture phone, they had just come out. I was SUPER COOL that day) I thought it would be really funny to include some of the topless pictures of myself from earlier, without telling him.

The sun was getting low and it was starting to get cold. We said our goodbyes as Orange and I headed off into the sunset aka to Orange's friend's house for dinner. Once there we ate, drank wine, laughed and then we snuck into the bathroom together to "refresh our makeup." I set up our makeup station as Orange sat down to take a piss.

That's when it happened. I will never forget.

At the very moment I was snorting up my pixie dust, Orange tooted! Along with my magical powder, I took up my nose that night the smell of her garlic eating, wine hangover and Mexican lunch having, ginger anus.

I had never felt my gag reflex so strong in my life.

Bitch.

The next morning I awoke far too early to my phone ringing. My body felt like I had fallen off of a balcony. I looked at the caller ID and as soon as I saw that it wasn't work, denied the call. A second later, my phone rang again. Again, call denied. It rang a third time. Okay, someone was REALLY trying to get a hold of me.

Was it that hot guy from the Internet I slept with last week who never called? Could it be Orange in trouble and needing my help? I figured I should probably answer.

"Hello?" I said.

"Is this *****?" a female voice asked me.

I paused, "Uhhhh, yesssss."

"You know Carlos?" she asked again.

I thought for a moment, in my eye shadow recovering haze. Quick flashes of the last several Saturday nights passed through my mushy brain. Nope, I was certain. I didn't know any Carlos.

"No, sorry. I don't know anyone named Carlos," I responded.

"You don't know Carlos?" she asked me, starting to get annoyed.

Again I said, "Nope, sorry."

I was pretty damn sure I hadn't boinked any Mexicans in the last few months.

That's when it happened.

"YOU STUPID FUCKING WHORE! You sent my boyfriend naked pictures of your ugly, skank self and then you pretend like you don't know him?" she yelled at me.

She seemed mad!

I still wasn't quite catching on, she continued, "You have blonde hair and an ugly, tramp tattoo of a fucking horse! I know what you look like! Are you listening to me, Bitch? I'm going to find out where you live and then I'm going to cut you!"

Uh oh!

I hung up the phone. Then it clicked. The gays... THEY WERE NOT GAY! They never said they were gay, they didn't hold hands or anything.

OOOOPS! Hahahahahahaha!

My phone rang again. I picked up, "Hello?"

"Don't you fucking hang up on me, Whore!"

"Hey listen," I began, "You are talking about the gays from the beach. I only met them once and..."

She cut me off, "GAY! You know damn well he ain't gay when you was fucking him! STUPID, LYING SLUT!"

I hung up again and tried to dial Orange but I couldn't, the girl was still calling. I denied the call.

Ring!
Deny!
Ring!
Deny!

This bitch was CRAZY! After roughly five minutes, I turned off my phone.

I tried to go back to sleep but it was useless. Instead, I crawled out of bed and into the bath, I had work in a few hours anyway. After my bath, I bravely turned my phone back on. My voice mail box was full. Just as I was about to listen to my messages, the phone rang. It was HER!

Phone, off!

I went to work and a few hours later, I hesitantly powered on my phone.

THE CRAZY BITCH WAS CALLING AGAIN! She called through my entire nine-hour shift.

When I left work, she was still calling. I went out that night with the Fun Girls, all through dinner she called. She called 114 times in a row at one point. Not more than two hours total passed between her calls at the peak of her longest break.

It was the damnedest thing.

She called me non-stop for three days, I don't know how she found the energy. By the end of the third day, I had taken too much. Exhausted and overwhelmed I wondered if she had found my house yet. I was looking out my window, shaking. In public, I was looking over my shoulders. She wore me down. Nothing was going to stop her. I debated changing my number but I used it for work. That was to be my last resort.

Finally, I went to the police station. Officer Grant called the crazy woman back. I don't know what he said to her but it worked. She finally stopped calling.

Now, I want you know that I learned nothing that day. I have not stopped sending nudie pictures to strangers.

Although, I did stop snorting lines of cocaine when Orange was taking a piss, so, I guess there is that.

My Four Leafed Stalker

It has happened to even the best of us, beer goggles. You go out to a bar or club, have a few too many, and end up sleeping with someone you regret.

I pretty much regret everyone I have slept with while sober. You can imagine just what kind of beasts I have brought home under the influence. Some people are smarter about this type of situation than I was. Most people boink and bail. Not me, I invited a man to follow me forty miles home.

I woke up the next morning dehydrated with a headache. As I stretched my arms out and rolled over in my bed, there it lay.

A midget, in tighty-whities.

Now, I can not technically say that Loli-Pop was indeed a midget. At almost five feet tall, he was considered a normal man, physically. Although I am pretty sure he was also slightly retarded.

Now I know what you are thinking. Where the hell did I find this dwarf?

First off, he was dancing on a box at a club most of the night. He was in the air, I couldn't tell how short he was. Secondly, Loli-Pop was hanging out with one of my old friends so he could not be that bad, right? I found out later my friend didn't even know the little leprechaun.

Anyway, Loli-Pop awoke and was attempting to engage me in some pillow talk. Eventually, I was able to convince him to leave, but not until after he made me promise him a date.

The night of our date, Loli-Pop arrived to pick me up. He did not knock on my door, instead his dwarf ass stayed outside in his mammoth truck, honking his horn. Probably, I should have locked my doors and turned off the lights but instead I sheepishly went outside. I opened his truck door and stepped up into the passenger seat. There, in the driver's side, was my mini-man, sitting on a phone book. That's right, a phone book.

I looked over to discover Loli-Pop was wearing black leather booty shorts. His fuzzy miniature thighs were sloppily hanging out. He could barely reach the gas peddle with his pointed toes.

Once I shut the door, we were off. Loli-Pop was quite the gentleman. He offered me a tequila cocktail, in the car. I declined. This didn't stop Loli-Pop from enjoying his cocktail as he drove.

I was going to die.

The fear worsened as we approached the interstate. Loli-Pop was a terrible driver though we eventually made it onto the final freeway. There was a lot of stop and go traffic. That's when it finally happened, Loli-Pop hit another car. He pulled over to the side of the road.

"You go talk to the driver!" he ordered.

"What?" I gasped, "I'm not going to talk to him for you. You're the one that hit him!"

"I can't go over there in these shorts. I'll get beat up!"

Damn. Loli-Pop had a point.

I hopped out, exchanged insurance information with the other driver and assessed the damage. Loli-Pop was lucky that night, with the car anyway, not so much with me.

We made it to the club and paid the entrance fee. I went straight to the bar, while Loli-Pop climbed his dwarf ass onto a box to dance and stayed there all night. Yippee, I was freed, I ran into a friend that would drive me home. As soon as I could, I left without even saying goodbye.

Two days later, I was at work when I received the first surprise. A dozen long stem, red roses delivered. They were from Loli-Pop, but I never told him where I worked!

CREEPY!

There was a card, inscribed, "To my lovely lady, I look forward to my life with you."

What did this mean? Ewwwww!

I gave the flowers to a co-worker. When I arrived home that night, I found my second surprise. My answering machine was lit up.

I pressed play.

"*****, I came by to see you today but you didn't answer. You must have been at work receiving my little present. Call me so I know you got it," I hadn't given Loli-Pop my home number either.

DELETE! What a creep!

I looked out the window, half expecting to see a pot of gold. There was nothing there.

A few days went by. Loli-Pop continued calling, I didn't answer. He left several more voice mails requesting that I call him back and I deleted them all.

One night, after a long shift at work, I came home and poured myself a glass of wine. Immediately after, like a horror film, it happened. There was a knock on my door. My dog started barking as I looked out the window. It was Loli-Pop! I silently walked into the kitchen, hiding myself from the windows. The knocks continued and they were getting louder. That was when the yelling began.

"*****! I know you are in there, I saw you. Please come out and talk to me, Honey! What did I do?"

Knock, knock!

Knock, knock!

Knock, knock!

Bark! Bark! Bark!

"Baby, please let me in or at least come outside."

Knock, knock!

Knock, knock!

Knock, knock!

Bark! Bark! Bark!

"Princess, stop hiding from me."

Now, I know what you are thinking, "How can you be afraid of a little man?" You think I am a pussy! I will have you know, I've seen horror movies about this kind of thing and I am fully aware what the miniatures are capable of.

It's a damn good thing I didn't go out there. Loli-Pop was a bit unstable.

Knock, knock!

Knock!

Knock, knock, knock!

Bark! Bark! Bark!

"You fucking bitch! Why are you doing this to me? Why are you hiding? You are a cheap slut! I can't believe I even fucked you!"

Loli-Pop was pissed. The harassment ensued for a good hour. I debated calling the police but I was too embarrassed.

All of a sudden, it stopped.

Thirty minutes later, my phone rang. I did not answer. The machine picked up.

"Hi baby! It's me. I went to your house tonight to see you but you must not have been home. Please call me when you get this," the little terror was trying to trick me.

Five minutes later, my phone rang. Again, I let the machine get it. Loli-Pop's voice mails were following the same pattern as his knocks. The more time that passed, the angrier he became.

"You God-damned whore! You led me on and now you are hiding like a coward!"

"Why wouldn't you open your front door? You will open the door to your love hole for me but not the door to your home?"

"I'll come back with wine!"

"You promised me your heart but instead you are smashing mine!"

I probably had twenty five messages by the time he called it quits, I did not sleep that night.

The next day I was paranoid. I was looking over my shoulders (Okay, under my shoulders) in fear of him following me. Luckily, he did not show up again. The next night he left a few, less aggressive voice mails. On some of them, he was even crying. A week later, he called me one final time. Then, just as quickly as it had begun, it ceased.

I hope he died.

Also, I hope that leprechauns go to their own special hell, a land where everything is too small for them.

Holiday Ho Down

I picked my son, PJ, up from his daycare on a Tuesday evening. After I signed him out, he grabbed his jacket. While we were walking out the door, PJ's teacher asked me, "Will PJ be at the performance tonight?"

"What performance?" I asked.

"The Christmas play he has been working on all month. I sent a flier home with him weeks ago!"

GULP!

Parental fail.

Immediately, I texted Pj's dad and grandma to inform them both of the event. Neither one could make it out on two hours notice. My son hadn't mentioned the performance to me, he couldn't be too excited about it, right?

I am an asshole.

So, I did what any guilt ridden, loser mom would do. I bathed PJ, put him in his holiday best and headed out to his show. When it was PJ's turn to sing with his class he proudly made his way onstage. The music started as PJ frantically began looking around, he was nervous because he could not find me. His face twisted in a way that I can only describe as my own.

Genetics have been cruel to my poor son because there he was, front row and center with a spot light radiating over his tiny body. He was standing there wearing his Christmas sweater while making MY nervous face.

Quickly, I jumped out of my chair and waved my arms at him. PJ finally saw me, his twisted expression softened.

He could finally relax, maybe he relaxed a little too much. The next thing I knew, PJ had bent down and was relaxing his bladder all through his Christmas pants. He sang on anyway.

Watching the children up on stage took me back to my own childhood. Of course it did! Everything is about me, after all.

I was a little older than PJ, maybe nine or ten years old and in the fourth grade. My best friend at the time, Christina, approached me at recess.

"*****, are you going to try out for the Christmas play after school on Friday?"

What was this Christmas play Christina spoke of? I hadn't heard of any play.

"I didn't know we were having a play," I told her.

"Yeah! Everyone is in it, singing in the chorus, but they are auditioning dancers for the 'holiday hoedown' scene."

Fuck. Yes.

"Are you auditioning?" I asked Christina.

"Yup. You can follow me to room twenty six for the audition," she offered.

Listen, even at age nine, I had no sense of direction. I could get lost in a playhouse.

Friday came and I was really excited. I was going to nail this audition and I was going to be the star of the Holiday play. This was my destiny.

After class, I followed Christina to the audition room. I signed myself in then took a standing spot in the middle of the classroom. The dance teacher put a tape in her boom box and pressed play.

"I'm going to demonstrate a few steps and then I want you girls to repeat after me, okay?" she asked us.

The class all nodded in agreement.

When the instructor started dancing we gracefully followed her lead.

Well, the rest of the class followed her lead. I had no rhythm or any idea what the hell I was doing. First, I bumped into Christina. The music was blasting, "Holiday! It's a holiday hoedown! Having a hoedown around the Christmas tree!"

Next, I tripped over myself and fell. Not only did I go down but I slammed into the girl to the left of me. It was like a domino effect. She fell into the next girl and so on.

The hos were going down!

One of the girls gave me a dirty look. I stuck my tongue out at her.

No matter, I was just warming up. I pulled myself up off the floor and continued on. Fall or not, I'm still fabulous!

Once the audition had ended, the teacher thanked us all for coming and told us that there would be a posting on the door of the classroom on Monday. We could check the paper for our names that morning to see if we had made the cut.

The entire weekend prior, all I could talk or think about was the holiday hoedown. I knew I would make it, I was destined to be a star. All weekend long, I annoyed my parents with non-stop hoedown jabbering. Christina grabbed her Bobbie Dolls and went home after an hour with me that Saturday. Even she had had enough hoedown talk.

Finally, it was Monday morning. I ran to classroom twenty six. On my way, I got lost but luckily ended up running into Christina. I followed that Bobbie bailing bitch to the door. There they were, written on cute snow flake paper, the winning names. My name was not on that list but Christina's was.

Bitch.

She was so happy that she was jumping up and down. I wanted to kick her.

One cold and snowy Idaho night, several weeks later, I was getting ready for the stupid play. After I put on the new dress my grandma had sent me for the occasion, I spent hours curling my hair in the bathroom. I plastered my 9 year old face in makeup. Even then I liked to dress up like a circus clown.

I went to the fridge to get out some apple juice for a quick drink before leaving when it happened. A giant bottle of cold, opened, sparkling wine came crashing out. On its way down, it spilled all over my dress. Then, it hit the floor and shattered. Wine and glass covered me.

My mom was in the living room watching TV.

"What the fuck did you just do? You stupid little cunt!" she screamed. She walked into the kitchen to see me there soaked and bleeding.

"That was my last bottle of champagne! I can't believe you just wasted it! You know I can't afford to buy more!"

"I'm sorry. It was an accident," I apologized, half heartedly.

"Why were you in the fridge to begin with?" she asked.

"I was thirsty, I..."

She interrupted me, "You ruined your dress. I hope it was worth it. Go change and get in the car, you are going to be late!"

I went into my bedroom and put on an old dress that had pink heart patches on it, my grandmother had recently sewn them on to hide the holes. Then, I got into my mom's car.

Mom was still angry and she was pretty drunk. Not a good combination when driving through a snow storm. We slid and skidded all the way to the school. My mom parked out front.

"Go inside," she ordered.

"Aren't you going to come and watch?" I asked her frantically.

"Ha, ha! No! I'm mad at you. Maybe your dad will watch. I'll send him to pick you up."

With that she grabbed the passenger door and slammed it closed, leaving me there alone in the snow.

"Fucking Bitch," I muttered while crying.

Quickly, I regained control of myself, wiped my tears and made my way into the school. I followed my class onto the stage. The lights went out, the music started as I watched the curtains open. The children all started singing, except for me. I just stood there with my arms crossed and my lips pressed shut for an hour.

Then, it was time for the "holiday hoedown." I saw Christina and the other lucky seven girls dancing on stage in their new, sparking pink, cowboy boots. They had huge smiles on their ugly faces.

I hate them.

Once it was over, they joined the rest of us in the choir for the final number. Just then, I saw my dad and brother walk in. With no seating left, they stood on the side and waved at me.

I smiled for the first time that night. The show ended a few minutes later. My dad took me home.

In the car, on the way back to our apartment, my dad said to me, "Don't worry about not making the cut for the 'hoedown.' You had the best voice in there. I could hear your singing above everyone else's!"

I did not bother to tell him that I hadn't opened my mouth once, that entire night.

I am a terrible singer anyway.

Real Friends Help You Move Grenades

By now, you are probably wondering why the hell Red has continued her decade long friendship with me. Why she would put up with my bullshit after all these years. Well, I will tell you why. It's simple really, crazy attracts it's own. Underneath Red's calm demeanor is hiding another psychopath. That's right, one time Red almost blew us up.

It all started when Red's husband, Skillstorm, found a job overseas. He left a few months prior to Red. This left Red with the task of moving their entire apartment, alone. Red being the procrastinator that she is, waited until the last weekend to get started. I just so happened to be in town that fateful weekend, so I helped her out (after a day of partying, anyway).

Saturday morning, after a few mimosas, I pulled up to Red's apartment and walked into the disaster from hell. There were boxes, clothes, trash, dishes (you name it) everywhere. In the center of it all, a giant trash can.

I loved this.

You see, being OCPD, I am the opposite of a hoarder. I hate clutter, I hate mess. So, I throw everything away. This can cause many problems when I am searching for important documents or bills. Plus, I had wanted to trash most of Red's apartment our entire friendship.

I was in bliss!

Red was not alone in her apartment that day. She had two of Skillstorm's friends there helping, a delightful couple named Cherry and Boots.

Immediately, I started doing what I do best, throwing stuff away and ordering people around. I'm not really sure what I liked more. Throwing stuff away or ordering people to throw stuff away. Red didn't mind, she was numb to my antics and grateful for my help. Cherry and Boots were also good sports.

"Throw it away!" I ordered, "Throw it all away!"

My eyes were sparkling. However, there was one thing we could not dispose of that day.

Boots grabbed a bag off the hook of the bedroom door. He opened the bag up and looked inside. Gently, he set it on the bed and whispered, "Oh, shit."

Seeing his actions, the rest of us paused.

"What is it?" Cheery and Red asked in unison.

It was a live grenade.

You see, a decade ago, when Skillstorm was discharged from the Marines, he decided to take with him a little souvenir. It was a small, but still explosive, souvenir which he kept in a bag hanging on the bedroom door, until today.

The four of us stood there, still, trying to decide what to do. We couldn't put it in the trash in fear we would blow up the trash man.

After a few minutes of debating, Red came up with a plan. She would call the fire department and ask where we could drop off explosives. You know, anonymously.

This sounded like a great idea to the rest of us.

So, Red did what any scared, rushed, explosive concealing ginger would do. She picked the grenade up with salad tongs, placed it between two bricks on her porch and made the call.

Can you guess what happened next?

No, luckily the grenade did not explode. However, as it turned out, the state of California did not have anonymous bomb drop off centers. Nope! As a matter of fact, we were then considered terrorists in the eyes of the State.

Yippee!

Within two minutes the sheriff, the fire department and the bomb squad had arrived and blocked off Red's entire street. Red, being the ever courteous neighbor she was, knocked on apartment doors, one by one, trying to explain the situation and apologize. This was a silly thing to do because they EVACUATED THE ENTIRE APARTMENT COMPLEX!

She could have, much more easily, apologized to everyone all at once, as they huddled outside waiting to get back into their homes for those four hours.

Red is an asshole.

She sat outside by the caution tape being interrogated for what seemed like hours, she deserved this. To add insult to injury, her brother showed up to help just in time to witness the event. Her father arrived shortly after. Both relatives enjoyed this very much. Why, it was a full humiliation for Red. Her face matched her hair.

The law took pity on Red that day, she did not get sent to prison. After several hours, it was decided that the grenade was not an imminent threat, so the bomb squad took it with them. The caution tape was removed and we were all allowed to reenter the apartment to try to finish up the big move.

Friends help you move but REAL friends help you move hand grenades.

Somewhere Under The Rainbow

    I spent the last St. Patty's day in Washington DC. The man I was dating at the time flew me out first class. We toured the city on foot by day and by driver at night. The white house had colored their fountain festively green to be in the spirit. It was an amazing trip.

    I was sent home alone, but it was first class so who I was to complain? Instead of my companion, the seat beside me was given to a young black man. He sat in his seat looking straight ahead almost the entire trip, only rising to let me out of my window seat as so I could empty my ever-filling bladder.

    Anyone who has flown first class is of course aware of their complimentary, endless wine service. Well, that and their hot nuts. Where else besides the Lit Fart can you get your mouth on endless warm, salty nuts free of charge?

    It was a five hour flight. By the time we landed I was already toasted and bored, a dangerous combination. So, I did what any annoyingly drunk whore left alone on a first class flight would do. I reached over and told the poor man sitting next to me the "Leprechaun Story."

    Now, before I begin, I must admit that I have butchered this story horribly. I was wasted the first time Red told it to me and I was wasted retelling it. Pretty much every time it comes out of my mouth it changes a little. Enjoy!

    ~Somewhere, in some small town in Scotland, there lived a friend, of a friend of my friend, Red. We shall call her Sara.

    Sara was throwing a weekend bash with her husband Aaron. Their party started on a Friday night and kept its fun going well into Sunday. By Sunday evening, Sara was ready to wind it down. She was a school teacher and she had a class to teach Monday morning. Aaron, in his drunken state, was not ready to end the party. He didn't have to work that next day or all week for that matter. Aaron had been laid off.

Sara went to bed late that night. When she awoke, early that next morning, Aaron was still partying. She got dressed and went to work anyway, already annoyed. While on her lunch break she received a call from Aaron,

"Sara!" Aaron slurred, obviously still on his bender, "You must get home immediately, you won't believe it! I caught a leprechaun! Our days of suffering are over!"

Sara was not pleased. She was very annoyed and ticked off at Aaron. He obviously STILL had not slept.

"Aaron, go to bed now. I'm warning you, if I come home and the party is not over there will be hell to pay."

Several hours later Sara's work shift ended and she returned home to find the party was still in full swing. She went on a hunt for Aaron. He was standing in the kitchen.

"Sara! Come over here and look at this. It's a leprechaun!" Aaron shouted, excitedly.

That's when it happened. Aaron opened the door to the kitchen cabinet and exposed a little boy with Down Syndrome. He was shaking while clenching his wee backpack.

You see, not far from Sara and Aaron's house is a school for mentally challenged children. Aaron had snatched his good luck charm early that morning while outside waiting for his little yellow bus.

Sara stared on in shock. When it finally hit her, what had occurred, she loaded the boy into her car and quickly dropped him back off where he had been found.~

What a festive St. Patty's Day story, right?

My co-passenger did not think so. He blinked a few times before he slowly turned his head to face me and said, "What is wrong with you? Someone must have had too much to drink."

"Perhaps," I mumbled, ashamed.

Then, he turned back his head to face the front of his own seat.

We didn't know it yet but our plane was just about to have an hour delay at the gate. Talk about an uncomfortable silence.

Douche.

Skewer Through The Heart

Guess what time it is? It's peanut butter, jelly donut time!

Before I lost the game to Donut that second time around, I actually had the lead for a little bit. That's right! I had learned a few tricks and beat him at his own game, if only for a moment.

I watched my little red avatar jump off a stack of bricks with his fist in the air. He grabbed onto a flag at the top of a pole and slid down. Five thousand points, I was going to the castle.

Donut and I made Thursday night "our night" to hang out. After roughly a month of this, with some planning, we found a weekend we both had off of work and without kids.

I wanted nothing more in the world than a romantic weekend alone, naked with my puffed daddy.

I could not tell Donut though, he likes a challenge. Our conversation went like this:

Donut: "Friday night I'm going to a show. Saturday I'm going to the swapmeet. Either you can stay Thursday night and leave when I go to the show around six o'clock Friday evening or you can come by when I get home Friday night. Instead, you can stay until Saturday afternoon when I go to the swapmeet."

Me: "Hmmm, well I don't know. I was invited to (insert fake destination here) with my friend (inset fake name here). If you only want to hang out for one night, I might just be better off going on my (fake) trip."

Donut: "Oh. Well, I guess maybe I can try to get you a ticket to the show. I don't really think I can afford it but I don't want you to miss out on a trip over me."

Me: "Well, I would rather see you because the trip is kind of a hassle because (insert made-up problem here). But if you can not hang for more than one day I will go."

You get the point. I am the world's best manipulator.

This went on for about a day until I negotiated:
A full weekend alone with my little Apple Fritter.

Oh, my God! I was so excited. I spent that week floating on clouds.

The night before my heavenly, love shack getaway, I packed. This meant I stuffed as many whore-y dresses and stripper heels I could fit into an overnight bag. Okay, three overnight bags.

Thursday night finally arrived. I loaded up my car and then stopped at the grocery store. I bought Donut his favorite cheese snack, two bottles of cheap champagne and orange juice. We were going to have brunch together!
I had fantasized of this weekend for six years. I could not believe my dreams were becoming a reality and I knew Donut loved me because he bought me lingerie. No, I mean he bought me the expensive kind, costumes.
That night I got to play a dominatrix. I put on the tiny black dress, six inch hooker boots and a hat. Even though I pretty much sucked at the role, I looked hot.
I tied my deep fried daddy to his head board and then I spanked him and asked him if he loved me. He said, "Yes."
I put my finger in his donut hole.
Then, I did something really dirty. Yeah right, I am not telling you what I did this time, either. I cannot share these details of our ever binding love.
They are sacred to me because I love him. Plus, I was pretty drunk.
When I was through, I cut off Donut's restraints with his pocket knife. That was very stupid. Donut is lucky that I did not accidentally cut off an appendage.
I fell asleep in his arms.

The next morning, after waking, Donut filed me full of his cream. He was definitely, still in my top three, of the best sex ever.

We dressed, laughed and drank mimosas.

I put on the shortest shorts I could find. Donut watched, rubbed and complimented my legs. As a matter of fact, he even told me, "You have the best legs of any girl, ever."

Donut drove us to the swapmeet. They happened to be closed that day. No matter, he asked me if I wanted to BBQ instead, I did. We went to the grocery store. I picked out lobster tails, Donut picked out shrimp, onions and peppers for kabobs. We grabbed a case of beer, bottles of wine and all the fixings for mojitos.

Guess what? Donut even paid.

After we arrived back to Donut's shit-hole apartment, he lit the coals for the grill while I muddled the mojitos and served us drinks. We both went into the kitchen and prepared the kabobs together.

We make a great team in the kitchen.

Donut is the best BBQ-er that ever lived. The food was done. I was grabbing the plates and finishing up the melted garlic butter when Donut called me into the living room.

That's when I saw it. TV tray Sasquatch! Uh huh.

Donut had a fold up table hiding behind his couch! He pulled it out and opened it up for this very special occasion.

The food was amazing. Then, we played video games and had more sex.

The seafood, along with the cheese spread I brought, were pretty much the only things we ate that day. However, we drank all the alcohol.

It started to get dark and Donut suggested we put on a movie, I agreed. Poor Donut, he did not know that I had alcohol induced ADD. I could not just sit still and watch anything while intoxicated.

I rubbed Donuts feet and told him that one day, I would take care of him when he was old. Even, I would change his shitty diapers.

I WOULD!

Pretty much, I ruined the movie because I was an asshole. Next, I suggested we take a bath. Donut humored me. We crawled into his cracked, stained, tub together. He put on some music and I started bellowing along, horribly, while screwing up the lyrics. That's where my memory ends.

The next morning, I woke up in bed next to my precious, mound of dough. I smiled to myself when I saw him. Slowly, my hand crept under the sheets and into his boxers. Lightly, I stroked his cock. It was starting to get hard. He moaned before he opened his eyes.

"No!" he said, half whining, before rolling onto his stomach.

"What?" I asked, surprised.

"Leave me alone. Just go," he said.

OH FUCK NO! NOT AGAIN! NOOOOOOO!

I looked down at my wrists. They were fine. Phew!

Still, I seriously freaked out. I had an anxiety attack right there in bed. Uncontrollably, I was shaking.

"Wha...what, what did I do? I don't remember anything! Was it bad! Oh, my God! I did it again, didn't I?" I asked.

"UGH!" Donut said, "You weren't bad. You were just fucking drunk and annoying. You wouldn't go to bed and kept waking me up."

Half relieved, I reached for his cock again. Once more, he pushed my hand away.

Then Donut said something that morning that I couldn't believe. He said pretty much the worst thing ever. I want to smack him on his head right now just thinking about it, "You reminded me of my ex."

That mother fucker.

He also said at one point I tried to stick a BBQ skewer up his bum.

HA HA HA HA HA!

I got up, showered, packed my things and dressed for work. When I was through, I went to kiss my crumb cake goodbye. He wouldn't kiss me back, he wouldn't even open his eyes.

Purposely, I left a razor and body wash in his shower. Then, I went to work. I had the worst day, ever.

I tormented myself and drove my co-worker crazy. Desperate, I tried texting Donut several apologies. He just ignored me. As a matter of fact, Donut ignored me for three days.

I was devastated, again.

On the third night, I was out at the track, sobbing, running harder than I had ever run in my life when it happened, Donut finally texted me.

He said, "Look, I guess we can still fuck but there will be no more sleepovers. Definitely no more weekends together."

WOW.

I waited, I didn't even have to ask what this meant.

I ran a few miles more and I thought about what he had said. Magically, it happened, I grew gonads.

"I don't know, maybe," I finally replied, "I will have to think about it."

"What? What do you mean you have to think about it?" Donut was stunned. He was not expecting that. Donut thought I was his bitch.

I said, "I'll give it some thought. Frankly, I'm not sure I even want to see you anymore. Pretty much, you treat me like shit."

Donut was speechless.

That was it folks! I won that round, conquered the castle and fire-balled the dragon. This princess was safe, for now. It was on to level TWO!

The next time I stayed over at Donuts place my stuff was still in his shower. That sexy man was dough in my little hands, for another few weeks anyway.

That's The Spirit

I walked into the little dive bar on a Wednesday afternoon. The place was virtually empty except for two middle aged, balding men drinking cheap beer. In the corner, I noticed a heavy set brunette sipping on a glass of wine. After approaching the bar, I asked the bartender to speak to her manager. She pointed to the woman with the wine.

"Hi, my name is Ember," I said as I reached out to shake her hand.

She grabbed it and introduced herself, "I'm Coral. How may I help you?"

"I'm looking for a job," I replied.

"What are you wearing under your dress?" she asked.

"Thong panties and a leopard print bra."

"Perfect. You see that door? That's the changing room. I want you to go wait in there. When the next song comes on, follow the stairs onto the stage and strip down to your bra and panties."

So, I did.

I waited behind the stage for the next song, bottled up all my courage and took my perfect, 5'8", 125 pound, natural C cup, 21 year old self onto that splintering stage. I had never spun on a pole before, and it showed. Still, I got up there and danced like I was in a music video, only without any rhythm. This was my first trip to a strip club and I had no idea how to act sexy. Although I was young, naive and awkward, I was still really hot.

I needed the extra cash, so I took the job.

This wasn't a normal strip club. This was more of a burlesque club. It was classy for a dump. I never had to do a lap dance. Not until the big clubs in Las Vegas anyway. My wages were earned in the form of a weekly paycheck, "one dollar bill" tips thrown onto the stage and the bean burritos a cheap customer used to bestow upon me on a regular basis.

I was a cocaine infused, neon red extension wearing, hopeful little slut with a plan. That day, I found the nearest stripper store and bought myself a new wardrobe. My favorite piece being a sheer, blue sequenced bikini that resembled dental floss, more than anything else. I bought several pairs of eight inch heels. Black ones, red ones, clear ones...

I paused, with my eyes gleaming when I saw it. Sparkling as it mechanically turned was a jewelry case. Only, there were no earrings inside. Displayed in all their glory, there they were, titty pasties. They came in all shapes and colors. I asked the clerk to open the glass and I excitedly chose several perfect pairs of nipple covers. That's right, I bought silver sequined stars, black leather circles, you name it. They even came with their own little tubes of eyelash glue to hold them on.

At check out the clerk asked me if I wanted to purchase Spirit Gum. That was strange. I didn't need any stupid gum. Was she trying to tell me that I had bad breath? She was just trying to up-sale me, I figured. After I had completed my purchase, I headed to the club for my big night.

The bar was crowded as I made my way through the entrance. Once inside the dressing room, I carefully picked out my pasties. I decided upon the black leather pair, applied the glue and stuck them onto my little strawberries. Next, I pulled on a pair of black vinyl short-shorts and a matching top that resembled a belt. After I was dressed, I clocked in and headed up to the bar. I ordered two, double greyhounds and slammed them back to back.

Then it was time, my first REAL striptease.

As the song of my choice began playing I made my way up to the tiny stage. I climbed the stairs and opened the curtain, shaking.

"Focus!" I yelled at myself. I was dreaming of easy money (though I probably never made more than $80 a night at that dump), I saw dollar signs. Plus, I was already buzzed. Pffft, I could do this!

I clanked my half drunk, 8" stiletto wobbling, whore self across the splintering stage and over to the rusty pole, I gave it all I had. My hand grabbed onto that sucker as I began gyrating my hips. The crowd loved this. Slowly, I removed my belt of a top and swung it around before dropping it onto the filthy floor. Men were throwing dollar bills onto the stage. So, I got on all fours and crawled over to retrieve the beginnings of my fortune.

That's when it happened, PLOOP!

My right pasty popped off and into the crowd. I covered my exposed milk jug with my hand. One helpful, overly excited, sweaty pig of a customer picked it up and handed it back to me. He grabbed my hand a little as I took it from him.

Ewwwwww.

I scurried back stage and glued it on again as fast as I could. After all, I still had two more songs left in my set. Once it was secured, I climbed back onto the stage. My second song was starting and I was gaining confidence, I was a pro. Smiling widely, I began spinning circles on the pole. Loudly, I could hear the crowd cheering, they liked this. The more I bounced the louder they got.

That's when I noticed it. Both pasties were missing in action. Uh huh. The crowd wasn't cheering because of my fabulous dance moves, they were excited that I was naked from the waist up.

Suddenly, the music stopped.

"Get off the fucking stage, Ember! Get your tits in check! Farrah, you are up!" It was Coral, she was pissed.

I put my arm over my tatas, collected my top and tips and clanked off stage. Farrah bumped me on her way up.

"Skank!" she whispered under her breath.

When I climbed back down into the dressing room, Storm, a thirty-something, chubby blonde dressed as a gypsy took pity on me. You see, the state had very strict laws on the type of nudity that could be shown at bars and I just unintentionally crossed the line. I could have caused the bar to be heavily fined or worse, shut down.

"Ember, what do you have holding your pasties on?" Storm asked me.

"The glue that they came with!" I exclaimed, still out of breath.

"Honey, you need to purchase a glue called, 'Spirit Gum.' That shit they come with doesn't hold, as you have noticed." she lectured. Then she handed me a tube of her own.

"Use this tonight and then tomorrow, go buy some."

DOPE!

That was what the clerk at the stripper store was trying to tell me!

Thus began my entrance into the land of burlesque stripping. Donut liked strippers.

Toys For Sale

While in my early twenties there lived the most annoying child there ever was. He was in the apartment next door to me. I never knew his real name, I called him, Toys For Sale.

Toys For Sale earned his name rightfully so, by loading up his rusty red wagon with dirty stuffed animals, GI Johns with missing legs, naked, headless Bobbies and any other scrap toy he had hanging around his ghetto apartment. He would then walk through the neighborhood sidewalks early in the morning shouting, "Toys for sale!"

He did this on a regular basis. It woke me up several times.

Early one Saturday morning, while still up from Friday night's bender, I devised a brilliant plan to seek revenge upon my young nemesis.

I, along with whatever sucker was hanging with me that night, started by filling up a giant trash can with water balloons. We spent a few drunken hours piling them up one by one in the kitchen sink. There must have been close to two hundred when we finished. We then dragged them out onto the balcony just as the sun was coming up. Plot prepared, we waited.

Sure as shit, at six in the morning, we heard it. The eight year olds screeching voice, "Toys for sale!" he sang along to the squeaking of his wagon wheels.

Sneaking out onto the balcony, we assumed our positions.

Ehh-ehh! Ehh-ehh!

It echoed down the alley.

As soon as Toys For Sale rounded the corner and was directly beneath us we let loose. That's right. We dropped those water bombs as fast as we could. The poor kid didn't know what to do. I loved this.

"Ahhh! Stop!" he whined.

We just laughed and kept chucking them. He finally got the hint and started running. I almost pissed myself but I kept throwing.

SPLAT!
One landed by his foot and splattered his clothes.
SPLAT!
Another landed on the back of his thigh soaking him, he ran faster!
SPLAT!
That's when it happened.
A balloon landed on the back of his neck with full force knocking him down to the concrete. He slid on the water across the cement skinning his face. We had gone too far.

With drunken speed, we ran our asses back into the apartment, closing the door and shutting the blinds behind us. We waited for the sirens, breathlessly, sure that we were going to be arrested.

The police never came.

Poor Toys For Sale. His drug addicted parents didn't even care.

One point: Drunken Skank.
Zero points: Toys For Sale.

All Dogs Go To Heaven, Even Retarded Ones

I hate dogs and I shall tell you why. Besides the obvious, they stink in general, their breath is even worse. They drool, shed and bark. They whine. They dig. They jump. Some bite. They eat trash. They eat shoes. The list goes on.

Mostly, I hate dogs because all dogs remind me of Rita.

I spent a few years living alone in a ghetto apartment. After a break up which resulted in a restraining order against my ex boyfriend, Pepe, I awoke one morning to loud pounding on my front door. The knocking was soon replaced by shouting.

"You fucking bitch! You stupid, fucking bitch! I'm going to kill you! You whore! I want the rest of my God damned shit!"

Then, I heard glass break.

I looked out the window and saw him. My ex, Pepe. Uncontrollably shaking, I called 911.

Now I don't know if you have tried to call 911 on a cell phone but it does not go smoothly, especially when you are dialing from a phone that has an area code in a neighboring city. Ten minutes and three transfers later I was connected with the right office and police were dispatched.

By the time the police arrived, my porch had been vandalized and my garage in the back of the complex had been kicked in. Pepe was long gone. Besides myself, there were no witnesses. Basically, there was nothing the police would do.

I was terrified, I didn't sleep for days. At night, I laid awake just waiting for him to come back. Would he kill me this time? He had already been arrested for trying.

So, after almost a week of sleepless nights, I did what any scared shitless, twenty two year old female would do, I went to the shelter and adopted a dog (I considered a gun, but really, do you think that would have been a better plan?).

I was guided through the halls by a hefty man on staff as I looked from cage to cage. Mostly, I liked the big male Pit Bulls. They were not eligible for adoption. Also, I liked a huge Rottweiler, probably not the best dog for an apartment. Then, I saw her and that mushed up, lopsided face.

She looked Pit Bull enough. The guard said she was a mutt. Probably some American Stafford, some Boxer, but who really knew. She was roughly around two years old and a good candidate for adoption. Next, I was escorted into the meeting room to wait for the dog to be brought in.

I hadn't noticed it from the cage but the dog was malnourished. She was all head and ribs. Also, she had a collar that was on so tight, it was cutting into her skin.

That's when I saw it, huge, dangling nipples.

These things were hanging down literally an inch from dragging on the floor. I was told this dog had been picked up without her puppies two days prior and had obviously just given birth. Most likely, she had been used to breed fighting dogs then abandoned after. This dog was a hot mess. I couldn't leave her there. She was scared, scarred and shivering.

Later that day, I signed the papers, paid the fee and off she went to have her shots, be spayed and micro-chipped.

I picked Margarita (Rita for short) up from the pound two days later. She was high from the anesthesia and wobbled to my car. When we arrived to my apartment, she was still a bit unsteady. So, I made her a bed on the floor before heading to work.

When I arrived home that afternoon, she was still in her bed but had started to come around. She stood up and wagged her tail obviously grateful to be rescued. I took her for a walk and she relieved herself on a patch of grass. That was probably the last time she saved a load for outside.

You see, Rita had to be the most retarded dog that ever lived. I must be the biggest sucker for the mentally challenged because I always end up in situations caring for them.

In the years that followed, if I walked out of the house without Rita-tarded, she would whine and bark. Then, immediately, she would relive herself onto my carpet. It didn't matter if she had access to the backyard or not. She would climb onto my bed and drool all over my pillow. The damn thing shed everywhere too.

Rita did the usual, daily trash digging. She ate all my shoes and even learned how to open the closet door to get to them. Also, she destroyed everything in her path.

She was like a hooker with AIDS.

One day, a year after her adoption, I was physically assaulted by my newest boyfriend and instead of rescuing me, Rita hid in the bath tub, with her tail between her legs. The dog was useless.

Around the same time, I remember, attempting to microwave turkey sausage for breakfast. It didn't turn out well at all. I wasn't going to eat it, so I gave it to Rita who ate it in one gulp. Immediately, she threw it back up onto the carpet. I went to retrieve cleaning supplies and when I returned the mess was gone. That's right. She ate it again. Very disgusting.

So, I did what any fed up, retarded dog adopting asshole would do in my situation. I put an ad up online for a free dog along with a picture. No one responded.

The years came and went and Diah-Ritas behavior worsened, I had kept her out of guilt. I despised the damn thing but she loved me. It was horrible, I continued to post ads for a free dog.

Four years later, I was living alone in Las Vegas with my son. I was married and pregnant with my daughter. Beans had not yet committed to moving in with us.

Every morning I was picking up giant logs of dog crap off my dining room floor. I was mopping huge puddles of urine up as well. The smell was rancid and I was having morning sickness. It was in itself, unbearable. The dog was getting into my son's room and destroying his toys one by one. She was dragging the trash can around and spreading waste everywhere. My son and I were always covered in dog hair. Plus, I was getting tired of beating it.

Roughly, four months into that pregnancy it happened, the final straw.

I was in the kitchen making dinner when my son walked in. He had something in his hand and he was eating it. What was it? A toy? No. Chocolate? No.

"That's strange," I thought to myself, "I didn't give him anything to eat."

I pulled it out of his hand and examined it. It was cat poop. Uh, huh. The dumb dog had wedged herself between the two couches and under a coffee table, into the covered cat box. The opening had been facing a wall yet she still managed to pull out the turds. After eating her fill, she left the rest of the treats on the carpet, for my son to enjoy.

This bitch was now messing with my child's health. She had to go. I spent the next few nights calling every no-kill shelter in town but none would take her. They were all full due to the housing foreclosure nightmare which was currently ravaging Las Vegas.

So, I did what any guilt-ridden, pregnancy hormone riding pussy would do, I made Beans handle it.

The following weekend, as I headed out to California with my son, I left Beans and Rita alone in my apartment. I removed Rita's collar and threw it in the trash and said my goodbyes.

I was in California on Saturday afternoon, working my part time gig in the salon, when my phone rang. The caller ID said it was the shelter, I did not pick it up.

You see, Beans had actually found a no-kill shelter that was willing to take Rita that day, on one condition, she had been fixed. However, Beans and his five brain cells decided to lie. He told them that he had "found her," thus could not prove that she had had the surgery. So, the no-kill shelter, not being able to obviously see her spaying scar, turned her away. Beans then went to the pound and dropped here there with the same story. Only beans did not realize one thing, Rita had been micro-chipped.

The shelter called my phone several times to come get my dog. I never called back. I am pretty sure I know the day she was put down, I could feel it. Plus, they stopped calling.

I will never own a dog again. Unless it's Donut's. I will gladly care for Donut's dog when we move in together.

Caution: Razor Is Scented

My entire life, things have happened to me that were a bit, "off the beaten path." I often wonder if these sorts of things happen to anyone else.

It has been a long time since I have had an orgasm. Being highly sexual in nature, it does not take much for me to get my rocks off. Once, on my way to Las Vegas, while wearing a pair of cut off jean shorts, I reached climax on Interstate 15, without ever touching myself. Go ahead, be jealous.

So, it was not too surprising that today, while driving home from Las Vegas, wearing my tight black jeans, that I got that sweet sensation. The vibrations of the car were delicate and teasing, the crotch of my pants was just binding enough and my thong panties wedged in just the right manner. I was almost in bliss.

I put on the cruise control and slipped on my giant sun sunglasses in an attempt to hide my sex face, or at least, my bedroom eyes.

Cruising along at a steady speed of 65 mph, it felt like I was riding an airplane through heaven.

First, I was thinking about Donut. Then, I was imagining that I was touching myself. The waves of pulsating pleasure were lasting a really long time. It reminded me of sex with Morthos.

That was the magic thought!

The one that was going to stain my seat! Then, just as I was about to make road kill it happened. Traffic. Fuck (and in the bad way)! As I slowed down my vehicle so did the vibrations. I lost my "big O." It was even more disappointing than sex with Brutus.

I had blue slugs.

Once I arrived home, I ran my horny ass into the bathroom and locked the door. I squatted on a rug after pulling my pants down to my knees.

I began tickling my navy bean. Once I was wet enough, I slipped my finger into my sloppy sissy and cleared out some cobwebs. Oh, my God! It had been probably years since I felt what it was like to have something enter me.

I needed more, I started looking around. To my left I spotted a pack of lady-shave razors. The handles were ribbed and thick. What a find!

As fast as I could, I ripped one out of the package and sat the head on the floor. I straddled the handle bouncing up and down, feeling every bit of the ribbing.

I was thinking about Donut. He was the last man to give me an orgasm. Oh, I wanted him BAD!!!!!!

AHHHHH! Finally: sweet release.

Once it was all over, I pulled the handle out of my filthy whore hole and inspected it. I giggled at the milky white mess I had left all over my make-shift dildo.

What was that appealing aroma? I put the gooey, rubber, rock-offer to my nose. It smelled so fragrant, floral.

"Wow," I thought to myself, "I must have the most pleasant vagina, ever."

The euphoric high stopped dead cold. That's when it hit me. Three letters: U.T.I. Oh, crap!

Who the hell thinks to put perfume on a fucking razor? Someone actually got paid for that! They consider themselves, genius! The razor goes in the shower, it gets wet. The scent disappears. I know this for certain because after I washed my crusted cunt cooties off the damn thing it didn't smell at all. I think the creator is an asshole.

Stop laughing at me!

I know what you are thinking, "Who puts a razor in their furbie to begin with?" You are also an asshole. I hate you.

Once I had this revelation of possible urinary track infection hell, this sexually experienced whore was knowledgeable enough to know what had to happen next. I sat down on the toilet immediately, to pee. Only, nothing came out. After a few minutes, I made myself poop. That always creates pee. It did, but just a drop.

The next day I went to the doctor to have my fourth UTI of the year cured. All of them had been for similar, stupid reasons.

Vaginal Volcano

It was a hot summer evening in Las Vegas. I was fifteen years old and living with my boyfriend at the time, Sandman. The two of us were walking back from a cigarette run. We decided to cut through an apartment complex. After reaching the end, we had a small wall to hop over. It was roughly two feet of bricks with another two feet of wrought iron on top.

I stepped onto the brick with my right leg. Then, just after I lifted my left leg over the wrought iron and was putting my weight down onto the other side of the fence, it happened. Sandman grabbed a hold of the fence to lift himself over. Only, he wasn't aware that the metal was loose.

WHAM!

160lbs of forced wrought iron slammed onto my vagina, "Ouch!" I screamed out in pain.

Sandman jumped over in shock, quickly apologizing. I hopped down and bent over holding myself. After a few minutes, with tears in my eyes, I stood up and limped back to our house. Once inside, I waddled my way into the bathroom to assess the damages. I pulled down my jeans and discovered blood. One side of my labia was torn and a little swollen.

I cleaned myself up and sat down in front of the TV trying to forget about what had just happened. After about fifteen minutes the pain still had not subsided, actually, it was getting worse. The hot burn would suddenly make a fast popping sensation that was followed by a horrible, deep sting.

I went back into the bathroom for another crotch check when I noticed it. In my pants was a little, bloody penis. My vagina was swelling up by the minute. The popping I was feeling was actually the blood rushing into my wound. It was literally filling the lip up, like botched injections.

I made my crotch an ice pack then soaked in a cold bath. My injury was worsening. I was starting to think that the emergency room might be a good plan. This meant that I would have to get in touch with my dad and I had not heard from him in close to a year. His roommate told me, on the phone, that he had not heard from him either, for at least a few days. Next, I tried calling my mom. She did not answer.

By the time I made it into the emergency room, I had a bloody appendage between my legs that was roughly the size of a baseball. Blood was even dripping from the bottom.

That's right, I had huge, oozing nuts. I could no longer wear pants. Instead, I had on a long skirt with no panties.

What a mess!

Sandman suggested I walk in the middle of the road and repaint the lanes red.

I waddled my way up to the reception desk and tried my best to explain what was happening to the nurse.

"Why are you here?" she asked.

"Ummm, well, I kinda.....I hurt my.....down there. I mean, I was coming back from the store and I hopped over this fence....it hit me, the fence hit me on, my....my vagina, its, ummm..."

Let me tell you, there is no smooth way to say, "My vagina is swollen and bloody. Except it's NOT my period." Well, I guess I could have said THAT.

Very embarrassing. Also, very painful.

The hospital staff finally understood what was happening to me, after all my screaming. Plus, it helped that Sandman was a little better at explaining the situation than I was.

He loved this.

The hospital staff led me into the examination room. I will never forget the look on that male nurse's face when he examined me.

Poor bastard.

I was immediately prepped for surgery. Being a minor, not having parental consent for emergency surgery, my case first had to be approved by a judge. The court order did not take long to implement. Soon, I was pumped full of painkillers.

Just as I was being wheeled into the operating room, I heard my dad's voice calling my name.

He was drunk, "*****! Oh, my God, *****! I came as fast as I could!" he slurred.

"Sir! Sir! You will have to move your car immediately!" a voice yelled.

A mask was put over my mouth.

"Count to twenty!" another voice said.

"I need to see my daughter!" my dad screamed.

"One. Two," I counted.

"You are blocking an ambulance. Move your car now!" the voice continued.

"Three," I whispered.

I woke up in the recovery room several hours later, alone. My dad had been sent home. Luckily, he avoided a DUI and he called me the next day to see how I was doing.

Sandman went home too. Then he scored an eight ball of crystal meth. I did not see him again for a month.

My mom had been on vacation at the Grand Canyon. Since I had to stay in the hospital for a week anyway, she didn't bother to cut her trip short.

A week later, after my release, I went home with my mother. The doctor who had operated on my bloated beaver told me that it was the size of a football when he had stared. I was internally bleeding and seconds away from having it rupture.

Vaginal volcano.

One afternoon, while spending half the day on the couch panty-less, in a loose skirt, I got up to have a little tinkle. After I released my bladder, I began limping back to the sofa. That's about when I saw it.

My mom was crouched over my sofa seat. She was trying to scratch away a dry, crusted white spot from the cushion that I had been parked at, with her fingernail.

"What is this?" she asked, "Were you eating on the couch?"

"No. Actually, I don't think that's food," I said, my face turning bright red.

She looked up at me.

I looked down at my crotch, "I can't really wear panties right now," I stated.

"Oh, my God! That's disgusting! You are fucking sick! What is wrong with you?"

Ha ha ha ha ha!

"I'm injured!" I yelled back at her, in my own defense.

She ran into the bathroom to wash her hands.

I was assigned a towel.

After a week at my mom's house, I was driven back to Sandman's. I waddled into my room to find it filthy and destroyed. My pictures had been torn up, fish were missing out of the aquarium, the walls were dirty and weird chemicals were strewn everywhere. Sandman was nowhere to be found.

Holy hell! My room had been turned into a meth lab.

My sleep was shattered that following morning by someone running out of my bedroom and slamming the door. I looked to my night stand to see that someone had just stolen my pain pills. Seriously.

Sandman returned home that evening. His hair was greasy, breath foul and you could literally smell the drugs seeping out of his pores.

He hadn't slept since I went into the hospital. I told Sandman off while I threw things at his face. Then I called my dad, crying.

"Dad!" I whined, "This house is tweeker hell! I need to get out of here! Someone stole my pain pills and they destroyed my things while I was gone. You need to come and get me!"

"I have been drinking. Take some Tylenol. I'll come get you tomorrow," he said.

"No, Dad! You need to get me now!" I ordered.

"Damn it, *****! I told you already, I'm fucking drunk! Take a cab or wait until tomorrow."

"I don't have any money, dad!" I begged.

"That's not my problem."

CLICK

I had to get out of there. Immediately, I shoved some spare clothes into a bag and waddled to the curb.

Out went my thumb. A man stopped and I got into his car.

"Where are you headed?" he asked me.

"Henderson," I told him.

"Why? That's too far. How about you just come to my place for the night?" he suggested.

"Look, I just got out of the hospital. I'm in pain and I need to go home."

The man reached over to me and began fondling my chest. I slapped his hand.

"You don't want to go there, trust me," I warned, "You can't fuck me. I have a plum between my legs. I had an accident."

"Ya, right," he laughed before he started rubbing my thigh.

"I'm serious you pervert! Pull over! Let me out!"

The man lifted up my skirt and caught a glimpse of my swollen salmon. He was rightfully disgusted. The brakes of the car squealed, he leaned into me, opened the passenger door and literally pushed me out onto the street.

I was saved by the fruit of my own loin. I walked to the nearest convenience store and picked up the pay phone. Desperate times called for desperate measures.

"Hello?"

"Grandma! It's *****."

"Oh, Baby! I heard what happened. Are you feeling better, Honey?"

"No, Grandma. I have a purple plum between my legs. My room was destroyed. A tweeker stole my pain pills and then some man just tried to rape me. I called my dad and he won't pick me up. I'm stranded and in pain."

"What? Where are you at? You stay right there, Baby! I'm going to call that son of a bitch, right now!"

Forty minutes later, my dad pulled up.

"You little, fucking, sneaky Bitch! Get your ass in the car! Now."

I got in the car.

"I told you I was drunk! If you needed a ride so bad, you should have called a cab!" he screamed loudly, spitting as he shouted.

"Don't yell at me! I've had a shitty day!" I spat back.

"That's not my problem! It's your own damn fault. You should have just stayed with your mother."

"I didn't know Sandman would be fucked up!" I screamed.

"You didn't know that you lived in a meth house? You have been there over a year. Give me a fucking break."

"You are father of the fucking year," I mumbled.

"What was that?" he asked me.

"You are an asshole!" I shouted.

WHAP!

He hit me in the mouth. My lip stuck to my braces. When I detached it, blood trickled down my chin. I had him drop me at Grandma's apartment instead.

A few days later, I moved into my mom's house. Not long after that the stitches in my floppy flounder finally, fell out.

I mailed them to Sandman.

Luckily, I healed nicely down there, the skin just a little saggy. Baby meat curtains. No man has ever noticed, or perhaps cared. Once, I asked Beans if he thought I needed a vaginoplasty. As usual, he told me I was nuts.

Little did he know that I once had them.

Redbeard's Locker

I was sixteen years old when I moved back into my family's home. After recovering from my "vaginal volcano," I wanted to get on with my life. Plus, I needed to finish my education, I planned on having a bright future. With that plan in mind, I registered for school.

Because I was too far behind to be placed in what would have been my junior year of high school, I was sent to continuing education instead. You know, loser school. This school was designed to ensure graduation. The lessons were simple. I pulled straight A's and was usually bored out of my mind.

Then one day, something amazing happened. I was sitting in my math class when the door opened and tall, long-haired, hottie walked in. His name was Redbeard. Shiver me timbers. He took a seat in front of me. Then, he looked back and smiled.

My heart had just walked the plank. I smiled back. This corsair would be mine.

Redbeard was anything but shy. Right away he decided that he did not like our math teacher. He let the entire class know by loudly making fun of him on a daily basis. The teacher's feelings were quickly mutual. Our teacher found Redbeard to be loud, disruptive and assumed him to be a little dense.

Well, that is until he took Redbeard's reading material away. Redbeard liked to read for entertainment. The math teacher confiscated the book, probably assuming it was porn or comics. Then, when he discovered it was a book on Nostradamus, returned it. He had a new outlook on Redbeard after that.

A few days went by of Redbeard and me playing together at recess, if by playing together I mean making out and smoking cigarettes by the flagpole, when I did it. I asked Redbeard out on a date. That's right, even at sixteen, I was a direct, man-eating slut. Redbeard happily accepted my invitation.

    Our first date was Mexican fast food after school. As we ate our tacos and laughed, we discovered that we had some serious chemistry. Once we finished, Redbeard invited me back to his apartment.
    Together, we hopped onto the city bus and held hands the whole way there. After the two of us had arrived, Redbeard led me inside and into his bedroom. We joked, I giggled. Then, Redbeard kissed me.
    I had sea legs! That guy could make my whole body tremble and shiver with one touch. He had his hand on the back of my neck and lightly ran his nails through my hair while pulling my face to his.
    Redbeard had me ready for action in no time. This was something I had never felt before. I hadn't had much practice with my body. Everything was still new to me and I didn't know what I was feeling, but I liked it.
    Redbeard slipped his hand into my panties and started playing with my squishy missy. I liked this very much. In return, I reached in-between his boxers and his pants and kind of, touched "it." I was still shy, awkward and not really sure what I was doing. Plus, I was scared of weenies.

    I totally had a 1970's style bush. AHAHAHA!

    After, when his hand was covered in my vaginal juices, he decided it was time. He pulled off my panties, rolled on top of me and put his fire in my hole. I was having sensations I had never felt before. That's right, I was experiencing sexual pleasure.
    Yes, I had heard this was possible for a woman, but I didn't know how pleasurable it could be. Holy hell, I was having an orgasm. I don't mean five seconds of pubic bliss, either. I mean it was consistent. From the second Redbeard entered me, to the second he was done, constant orgasm.
    Redbeard showed me the mother lode. Quite possibly, the best sex I have ever had, to this day. Redbeard and I were inseparable after that, for a few weeks, anyway.
    He continued to swab my deck. Also, we started incorporating other things into our sexual escapades. One of

them being razor blades. Redbeard and I would take turns cutting each other.

I was in love.

However, I was only the second girl Redbeard had ever been with. As a matter of fact, he left the girl who had taken his virginity for me.

So, I did what any young tramp would do, when, in the beginnings of her blossoming relationship, with her fantasy man. I decided to test Redbeard's love for me. Uh, huh. I was going to make him tell me he loved me and I wanted him to chase me.

One evening, after Redbeard had careened my ship, I told him we should take a break.

"I know I'm only the second girl you have been with," I told Redbeard, "You are inexperienced. Maybe we should take a break for a while so you can explore a little bit. You know, just to make sure we are right together. I don't want you to feel like you are missing out on anything."

I gave Redbeard a concerned look. Then I waited for his response. He was going to tell me how silly I was to say that. After all, he loved me.

"You are right," he said.

What the fuck? Did I just hear him correctly? Our relationship was perfect! Obviously, Redbeard didn't think so. With that, Redbeard walked me out to the bus stop. He hugged me goodbye.

It was the longest bus ride ever.

The next morning I arrived to school. I saw Redbeard sitting with a group of our friends. He stood up and motioned towards me, I looked away and kept walking.

I ignored Redbeard in class.

At lunch Redbeard tried to sit next to me. I told him to fuck off before moving to the next table.

The next day of class, Redbeard was called on by the teacher. He gave his usual smart ass remark. Only, this time I chimed in, "Of course he doesn't know the real answer, he is mildly retarded."

Redbeard did not like this.

The teacher looked at me, stunned, "I thought you two were a couple."

"We were, before I knew what a bitch she was," Redbeard responded.

No way! Did he just say what I thought he did? It was on, Redbeard and I were at war.

Now, you may not understand how big this war was, it quite literally split the school in half. You see, Redbeard and I were the king and queen of all the losers, in loser school. Our classmates were literally forced to take sides.

I sat behind Redbeard in class. When he wasn't paying attention I reached into his backpack and filled it up with my open can of orange soda.

The next day, Redbeard took his revenge. Using a black marker, he drew a line through every blank piece of paper in my notebook before breaking all my pencils in half, while I was in the bathroom.

At lunch, I had one of my minions steal Redbeard's lunch box and hide it in one of the classrooms.

Redbeard retaliated by finding a test of mine on the teacher's desk that had not been graded yet. He changed all my answers.

I told the entire school that Redbeard had the smallest penis I had ever seen.

Redbeard told everyone that I had herpes.

We were sitting in class together, on a Wednesday. I was having a hard time with one of my assignments when Redbeard made a smug remark to me.

I was sick of his shit, that's when I did it.

I reached into my book bag, pulled out one of the razor blades we had used for fun and I sliced him with it across his arm.

Redbeard looked at me in shock. He stood up in class, with his chest puffed. Then, in the deepest voice he could muster said to the teacher, "I need to go to the nurse, I'm bleeding!"

My face was as red as the blood gushing from Redbeard's arm. I was certain that I was going to juvenile prison. There was blood everywhere.

"Shhhh!" I begged Redbeard.

"Why are you bleeding?" the teacher asked, concerned.

Redbeard looked down at me. I'll never forget the expression on his face. He really did love me, "I cut myself on a piece of wire from the fence outside and it won't stop bleeding."

Redbeard was protecting me, but the war was far from over.

He needed seven stitches.

Still I was obsessed with him and needed his attention in any form that I could get it. I could not believe he was still doing this to me. Why wouldn't he just apologize already? This was all his fault anyway, for not just telling me he loved me in the first place.

Then, one day, Redbeard didn't come back to class. At first, I was relieved. I needed a break from all the fighting and I was tired of watching my back.

A few days later, I was worried. I was starting to miss him. Plus, I was getting bored.

That was when I heard the news, he had dropped out of school. The war had ended, at school anyway. It continued socially for another year.

Sausage Island

Right now, I am waiting out my afternoon alone in a little Mexican restaurant. I have two hours to kill before my shift starts at work. This place reminds me of a restaurant I ate at while on a little California island early this year, waiting for the boat that would take me home.

Eating is a bit of an exaggeration, though. Really, I was drinking like a fish. I must have had seven Margaritas that afternoon, sitting there with Gruff and Jenny.

They were locals to the island. I had met them while visiting on my honeymoon a few years prior, with Beans. We had kept in contact. Since my divorce, Gruff and I had been "sexting."

Gruff had "the hots" for me and really wanted me to come and visit. I had been inebriated the one and only time I hung out with him. Though, I was fully aware of beer goggles by then, I still figured why the hell not. It was a free trip.

Gruff bought my boat tickets and a hotel room. He told me his friend owned the nicest hotel on the island and we would be getting the best suite.

When the weekend finally arrived, I took my hopeful, slutty, fake-breasted self to the boat dock and up to the ticket counter. I showed the clerk my ID and was given my tickets.

First class, free booze! Good job, Gruff!

I walked onto the boat and grabbed my complimentary cocktail. Ahhhh, mini-island vacation! I needed this.

After an hour of cruising the high seas, we docked. I walked my bubbly, buzzed butt off the boat and saw a hand waving at me. There was Gruff in all of his white trash glory.

"Shit. What I have done?" I asked myself.

"Oh well," I thought, "Jenny will be hanging with us too. It's not so bad."

Then, Gruff spoke. He had a voice like a robot. Twenty years of smoking had crept up on Gruff's vocal chords. I looked around for his voice box but there wasn't one!

Gruff had long shaggy hair and was shaking like he was on drugs. He was short, plus he had the biggest ass I had ever seen on a man. I'm sure it would make black women jealous. A rapper could probably write a song about it.

"Think positively," I reminded myself, "There will be more free booze."

Gruff thought that way too. Once we loaded ourselves into his car he handed me a bottle of champagne. Maybe Gruff wasn't so bad after all.

He asked me if I was hungry. I said yes, expecting Gruff to take me to a romantic restaurant. Instead he took me to the bank to cash his tiny paycheck. Then, he took me to a street vendor.

Once we bought our foil wrapped food we headed to the hotel. The hotel was very old and the courtyard was empty. Gruff unlocked the door and opened it to a room the size of a closet, barely big enough to fit a bed and TV.

Gruff popped opened the champagne. It was time for a toast, to me! I enjoyed this very much. I like it whenever anyone honors me. We both sipped out of our plastic cups.

Then, Gruff said he had to finish a little work and would be back in an hour, tops.

I checked out the bathroom. Not bad. It was actually a lot bigger than the bedroom and as a bonus, it had a hot tub. Perhaps I could live with this.

While I was waiting for Gruff's return, I decided that I would do a little shopping. After checking out the local over priced boutiques, I bought a few dresses and a giant straw hat. I wanted to look themed for the occasion.

As I finished wasting my money, I received a text from Jenny. She was coincidently in a shop on the same street. I stopped in and said hello.

An hour had passed so I figured I better get back to the hotel room to meet Gruff. I arrived to find that he had not gotten back yet. So, I sent him a text. He said it would be a little while longer still. I finished the champagne.

The hours passed and Gruff never came back. However, he did finally call. He told me to walk down to a local seafood restaurant and he promised to meet me for dinner shortly.

Once seated at the restaurant, I ordered a drink and waited. Then, I ordered another drink and an appetizer while I waited. I ordered a third drink, dinner and waited some more.

It was now time for dessert. I ordered a piece of pie, another drink and waited. Finally, I paid the check. That is when he showed up, apologizing. I was pissed off but also, I was pretty drunk. Though I should have told him off, I thought to myself, fuck it. I was only here for the night and it was already after ten o'clock.

Gruff and I headed to a local bar where we met up with Jenny and had even more drinks. I was tossed. Jenny was flirting with a guy she just met, Steve.

We all hung out until closing. The four of us, then walked back to the hotel room. Gruff, in his boxers and me, in my bikini, got into the hot tub. We invited Jenny and Steve to join us but they declined and instead made out on the bed.

After an hour or so, all pruney, we got out of the tub. I took off my wet bathing suit and put on a towel.

Gruff and I walked out of the bathroom to find Steve and Jenny almost naked on the bed. Again, I tried to convince them to get into the hot tub with us. This time Steve said yes.

So, I did what any drunken skank would do on an island vacation. I followed Steve into the bathroom and dropped my towel while peering down on his enormous erection. He saw me watching, smiled, and motioned me towards him. I sat on it.

That's right, I slipped Steve's big ol' "snake of love" inside me.

Gruff walked in, saw me screwing Steve, and exploded in rage. He grabbed a chair and smashed it against a wall, shattering it. Steve pushed me off of him and tried to calm Gruff down to no avail. Out of ideas, he grabbed his clothes and left. Jenny wasn't far behind.

After about a half-hour, Gruff finally calmed down and climbed into bed. I climbed into bed too. He touched my leg, I turned over and that's when I felt it.

Enormous wang. Gruff was packing.

So, I did what any girl not wanting to miss a second chance to get her rocks off would do. I hopped on pop and rocked Gruff's world. Then, I passed out.

I woke up that next morning disgusted and ashamed of myself, I walked into the bathroom and purged.

This woke up Gruff though he was in better spirits. In fact, Gruff was in love with me. He was so much in love with me that he already was comfortable being in my presence. By comfortable, I don't mean Gruff could "be himself," I mean Gruff was treating me like his wife. At least I think that was his mind set, because he kept blowing ass like it was an Olympic sport. Gruff was going for the flatulence gold. The sound bellowed out of his enormous ass like a sea lion in heat. I'm pretty sure he earned a medal that morning.

I needed to get the hell out of there, but my boat was not leaving for another three hours. So, I suggested that we go to the Mexican restaurant by the docks. Gruff told me that he could not afford it, he had spent all his money on my boat ticket and the room.

Out of necessity, I offered to pay. He texted Jenny and confirmed that she would be joining us, thank God.

That is when I started drinking. Three hours later, I was seven or eight Margaritas in. I paid the $120 lunch tab and then walked out towards the boat.

That's a lie, I stumbled onto the boat. Finally, I was going home.

I said my goodbyes and headed to the boarding area. The guard stopped me to inform me that I couldn't get on yet, I had to go to the end of the line and wait my turn. Gruff had sent me home coach. Cheap bastard.

The next day Gruff sent me an email telling me he had an amazing time and wanted to know when I would be back. I responded by telling him that I regretted the entire trip and that I would not be returning.

Gruff didn't take the dissolution of our "marriage" very well. In fact, he called me a cheap whore, a liar and a bitch. I'm sure I deserved it. Finally, I had to block his emails.

Poor Gruff. He doesn't know that there is only one man I will ever marry and his name is Donut.

Unhappy Ending

The last night I saw my little pastry prince was not a Thursday, but a Sunday night in late July. We had planned an overnight.

Donut was supposed to take me to dinner, as per our negotiations. I let him off the hook because I knew he was short on cash. He had just bought a new car and was a weekend away from moving into an apartment that happened to be a few blocks from where I currently lived. Plus, I didn't really give a shit about dinner. The negotiations were just a part of the little game we played for control.

As usual, I had on a hooker dress and six inch heels hidden under a big coat. I had given Donut a preview of this particular dress through one of the many dressing room photos I used to share with him.

Donut sent me a text telling me that he was off work and that it was time for me to come by. I headed out but made a stop at the grocery store for some beer and hummus, picking up Donut's favorite cheese spread, too.

When I was down the street from his apartment, I received a text from him asking me to pick up cigarettes. I happily did, I love doing favors for my love muffin.

Donut and I were still playing the back and forth/manipulation game.

I really wanted to stay the night with him but I had to pretend that I didn't care.

I sent Donut a text. The conversation went like this:

Me: Is there a street sweeper on your block Monday mornings?
Donut: I'm not sure.
Me: Well, I don't want to have to get up super early and move my car. I better just not stay over.

Then the most amazing thing ever happened. Donut was a gentleman. I'm not being sarcastic this time, either. My little, cream filled, pastry of love said something really romantic.

Donut: I'll park in the street. You can have my spot.

Can you believe it? Donut wanted me to stay. I arrived with the goodies. Then, something else amazing happened. He gave me money for my purchases.

Together we laughed, we played and we had some of the most unforgettable sex I've ever had. I'm sorry, I can't share. You know the drill by now.

Blah blah blah...LOVE HIM....blah blah DRUNK.

That night, I slept in his arms. When I awoke next to him that morning, Donut was still asleep. I debated waking him up but instead decided to play a move. Silently, I packed up my things and tiptoed to his rotting front door.

I was just about to make my exit when it happened, Donut spotted me. He walked in with his handsome, greasy hair disheveled and a huge erection peeking through his sexy boxers.

"You weren't leaving yet, were you?" he asked me.

I shrugged and blushed, "I couldn't wake you up," I lied.

Donut grabbed my hand and led me to his bed. He made sweet love to me that morning. When it was over, he cuddled with me, kissed me goodbye and he even walked me to my car. I didn't know it yet but that was Donut's permanent goodbye.

Donut planned on leaving me when he left his apartment. A fresh new start with a fresh new slut. He moved the following weekend to that apartment down the street from me. I offered him help moving but he declined, right before he canceled the plans he had made with me the following weekend.

So, I did what any obsessed whore would do when facing rough waters with her dream puff. I bought myself flowers, took a picture and posted it online where he would surely see it. Then, I made all my friends comment on the post.

Next, I went to a bar and made out with a stranger. I told Donut about it to make him jealous. Only, he didn't care. In fact he even wished me luck.

Though he wouldn't see me, Donut continued to flirt with me over text messages on a regular basis. One night, he ignored me for twelve hours straight, which was very unlike him. The following day, he had some bullshit excuse about leaving his phone at home.

I never made mention of his internet check-ins. However, he caught himself and tried to cover his tracks with an obvious excuse. Nope, I never did acknowledge any of it. Instead, I devised a plan.

I decided I would ignore Donut's texts for a few weeks to teach him a lesson. That's right, I was going to make him suffer. He would miss the shit out of me and I would take the lead again in our never-ending battle for control. I am brilliant.

Or maybe an idiot because my plan backfired. Donut only texted me for two days, just three texts total.

When I finally gave in and texted him a week later, he told me that he had met someone new. I was devastated.

First, I was angry. I told Donut off over fifty or so texts. I insulted him in every horrific way imaginable. He ignored me.

Then, I was sad. I confessed my undying love to Donut through another fifty texts.

He continued to ignore me.

Finally, after he couldn't take his phone being blown up anymore, Donut sent me a final text. It read, "*****, I don't want to be with you or date you anymore, we are through. I'm seeing someone else and I'm not going to blow it. That's it."

A couple months later, I told Donut I was ready to be friends and that's when he blocked me online.

I wish there was a book I could read for therapy on how to quit Donut, I guess there is, I'm writing it.

Super Sandman & The Hand Gun

  I was fourteen years old when I began my adventures of living on the streets, I didn't go home for almost two years. After a few months of couch surfing and food scrounging I met a shining prince. If by shining prince, I mean a tall, skinny, long, greasy haired, gap-toothed, methamphetamine addict by the name of Sandman.
  Sandman was a sweet kid, he really was. He just never had a chance. You see, his mother abandoned him when he was a child and he grew up in his father's crystal meth house.
  Sandman had never had a girlfriend before. He was smitten with me. I know this because he started doing for me something that he had rarely done before, showering and brushing his teeth on a regular basis. Although, he did not bother wearing underwear or clean socks.
  I particularly liked Sandman because he was pretty much the only guy I knew who hadn't already boinked my slutty friend, Butterfly.
  Sandman always wore basically the same thing. Black skinny jeans, black t-shirts and steel toe boots.

  Roughly, a week after Sandman and I met, I decided it was time to take his virginity. It happened late one afternoon. We parked outside a mutual friend's house in the ghetto. I wiggled out of my torn blue jeans. Sandman unzipped and pulled out his hairy, greasy, sour manhood and slipped that baby into my dried out whore hole. He was on top of me pounding away for the most exciting five minutes of his life.
  His sweat rolled through his hair and dripped onto my face. Yuck, I did not like this. Our socked feet bounced up and

down in the window. I know because our friends caught us and made fun of our "puppet show" for many years to come.

Once I let Sandman pop his "man cherry" with me, he was hooked. We started parking all around town and rocking his classic car.

One evening while parked under a freeway underpass, we huffed gasoline from a gas can and then humped like rabbits. The police caught us just as we were zipping up. We were lucky, they let us go with a warning.

Sandman wanted more of my sand paper poontang and he was tired of always risking it out in public (being a paranoid junkie). So, he did what any meth-addicted, horny, former virgin would do in his situation, he asked me to move in.

Since I was sick of living on the streets, I joyfully accepted and immediately called my parents. I hadn't talked to them since they threw me out earlier in the year. They were glad to no longer be responsible for me. As a matter of fact, they dropped all my stuff off at Sandman's.

We lived in a garage that was converted into a bedroom. The garage was disconnected from the house but had an attached laundry room. It did not have air conditioning. Instead, it possessed a tiny swamp cooler. The vent was not directed outside like it was supposed to be, but had instead been installed facing the laundry room. Whenever anyone would turn on the dryer, our room would turn into Florida in the summer, if Florida was in hell.

Also, it was infested with cockroaches. We would spend many nights spun out trying to rid the room of such nuisances. Did you know if you hold a lit flame to a cockroach they eventually explode and green slime squirts out? Very disgusting. You could have gone your whole life without ever having to know that. Have fun eating lunch now.

One night, while coming down off a three day tweek-fest, Sandman and I loaded into his father's car because Sandman's car was not working. After having spent several days spun out and trying to fix it, his car now resembled a telephone pole. It had countless wires streaming out from under the hood and stretching to the inside of the passenger window. A light switch from the house had been duct taped to the dashboard. Uh huh, it was being used as the blinker.

Tweekers are very creative. That being said, it wasn't actually functional.

Also in Sandman's father's car that day, were Bobby (a forty year old fellow powder sniffer and a friend of Sandman's dad who was living with us) and my good friend, Butterfly.

Bobby was driving while Sandman sat shotgun. Butterfly and I were in the back seat, chain smoking cigarettes. We were coming down off the drugs fast and desperate for a fix.

Once we had arrived to our destination, we pulled up in front of a gloomy and rundown portable home. A man was standing in front, on a dirt lawn. The man was Bobby's dope dealer, John.

Bobby rolled down the window to greet him. John whispered something to Bobby causing him to step outside of the car.

Then, Bobby started speaking loud enough for us to understand, "We are crashing hard, man. What can you give me for $40?"

"Let me have the money," John said.

Bobby handed him the cash. John slapped Bobby across his face.

We all sat there and watched silently.

"Where's the rest of it," John asked Bobby, "Why do you think I would sell you anything when you owe me money?"

Bobby started to speak once more, John slapped him again. Then, John reached into his back pocket and pulled out a hand gun.

He aimed it at me, "Get out of the car!" he ordered, looking me dead in the eye, "You too!" he said, moving his aim to Butterfly.

We obeyed, not wanting to be shot.

"You bring me the money and you can have the girls back," John told Bobby.

Then, he pointed the gun to the trailer door and told us to go inside.

Once inside we saw a woman, higher than a hot air balloon, sitting on a filthy, torn up floral couch. Next to her was another hand gun.

"You guys better wait in there for John," she said, directing us to a small room.

We listened and marched forward. There was nothing inside but a dirty, sheet-less mattress on the floor. The two of us sat down on that nasty thing and waited, both of us obviously terrified and trembling. I looked to the only window to discover it was nailed shut and covered in 2x4's. We needed a plan.

Silently, I reached into my purse and pulled out two pocket knives that I happened to carry on me just in case something like this were to happen. This was not the first time that I had needed them, but that's another story.

I handed one of the knives to Butterfly before opening up the other. Cautiously, I secured it in my palm.

"When John comes in you jump on him," I told Butterfly.

"I will! I'm gonna' kick him hard in his nuts! Then, you stab him!" Butterfly added.

We had our plan. It was go time, John walked into the rape room.

Butterfly turned to me, with a look that was asking, "Now?"

Before I could respond, John started to speak.

"You are two very lucky girls today. Neither of you know what I was going to do to you. However, that Sandman is a brave kid. His bravery saved you, his father happens to be a very good friend of mine. If Sandman hadn't spoke up about who his father was, I would have kept you. Bobby is a no-good, low-life snake. I wouldn't hang around him if I was you. You girls can go but first I suggest you say 'thank you' to Sandman."

With our miniscule weapons still in hand, Butterfly and I ran out of the torture trailer and got back into the car.

I don't even want to think about what could have happened that night.

My adventures with Sandman were just beginning.

Liar, Liar Zipper On Fire

I was twenty one, juggling three jobs (doing hair and managing a cosmetics line by day, burlesque dancing at night) when the call came in from my mother.

"Our house is finally finished, we are moving in a few days. I am selling the old one. Your brother is not moving in with us because he said he didn't want to. So, we didn't build him a room. Since we are selling the old house, he has nowhere to go. I thought maybe you would want to buy it and he could live with you."

Holy shit!

Was my mom really offering me my childhood home? I could not decline the offer, even if it was a three bedroom dive in the ghetto nor could I let my brother be homeless.

So, I did what any naive twenty one year old girl, looking to start a life would do. I quit all three jobs, packed my bags and moved from Los Angeles to Las Vegas two weeks after the invitation.

Once I arrived in town, I called my mom, "Hey mom, I'm here. Redbeard said I could stay at his place for a few days if I needed to. Were you ready for me to move in now?"

There was silence. Then, I could hear faint breathing on the other end of the line.

"What are you talking about?" my mom eventually asked me.

"The house, you told me to buy it from you and take care of my brother, remember?" I reminded her.

"I never said that, I thought maybe if you had a job out here first and saved some money I might consider it," she stated.

"That is not what you told me two weeks ago. You said you would let me stay there for a few months to get my feet on the ground first. I have an appointment for my Nevada, cosmetology license exam next month. I quit my jobs and I moved!" I screamed.

"That was before I talked to my husband and he said he didn't think it was a good idea. Besides, we already found a buyer."

I did not talk to her again for five years.

That was also the same time my on again/off again relationship with Redbeard ended. When it rains it pours. Redbeard let me stay with him three days. Then, he finally confessed to me that he had met someone else. He actually had just met the girl he would marry, but that's another story. I had to leave his apartment and I had nowhere to go. Up until that point, Redbeard was the love of my life, I was absolutely devastated.

Luckily, I had a lot of friends and I was able to couch surf but I still needed a way to make some money. Drunk, depressed and helpless, I did the only thing I could think of in the face of hard times, I started stripping.

First, I checked out some of the clubs. I found two of the least scary and started working. Being new to the club, I did not have seniority over the schedule. I was required work the worst possible hours, from four in the morning until noon.

Now, I had been dancing burlesque in Hollywood before this. I thought I had a heads up on how things ran. Stripping was not the same thing, it didn't even compare.

When I danced burlesque, I was on an hourly pay plus dollar tips from the stage. I had never done a lap dance before and had no idea what one entailed. My idea of stripping was spinning on a pole in pasties, not dry grinding in some perv's boner, topless, until he orgasmed.

I didn't make any money.

Not only did I not make money, I lost money. You see, when working for the big clubs in Vegas, one is considered an independent contractor. You pay to work. Then, you tip out the house. I ran up a huge bar tab every night trying to drown my nerves.

Something good did come of this, however. One night, while crying on the inside, I spotted the most beautiful, platinum blonde I had ever seen. She was heavier than I was but everything about her body was firm. Her skin was like porcelain, it radiated. She had zero cellulite.

Her name was Lady.

Lady walked up to me and sat down. She began speaking. Her voice was soft and sensual. We clicked right away. In fact, I was falling in love with her. That's right, a girl.

Lady also liked me and she showed me the ins and outs of the club. She was really into beauty and finding out that I was in the industry really excited her.

One afternoon, Lady invited me to her apartment and paid me to cut her hair. I was grateful for this because I needed some way to make a little cash.

While trimming Lady's hair I told her my story and how I was couch surfing. This upset her. As I was combing through her sweet, soft, baby fine hair the door swung open. A man walked inside, it was Lady's boyfriend.

"This is Pepe," Lady introduced us.

Pepe was tall and thin with arms full of tattoos. He was at least a decade and a half older than I was. Yet, his face was still riddled with teenage acne. He wore eyeliner like a rock star. Pepe really thought he was a rock star, he and Lady had formed their own band. They played a lot of shows and were actually fairly well known in Las Vegas at the time.

Pepe had big, twitching, blue eyes. He looked me up and down. Boy was he was a creep, through and through. I thought he was damn hot and Pepe thought the same of me. He used to always tell me that I was "out of his league."

As a matter of fact, Pepe and Lady asked me to move in that night. Then, something else happened. They asked me to be their girlfriend. I said yes.

I woke up in bed next to them one morning after I had been living there about a week. The sun was peering through the blinds. The bed was shaking, I rolled over and what I saw next scared the living shit out of me.

There was Lady, on her back, her legs up in the air resting on Pepe's shoulders. Lady was moaning. Pepe was penetrating her like a rabbit. He was making the ugliest sex face I had ever seen. Sweat and oil were dripping off his forehead.

Oh, my God. They were doing it!

I jumped out of bed and ran into the living room. Now, I know I said I would be their girlfriend but I wasn't ready to go all the way. I mean, I thought that there would at least be alcohol involved.

I sat down by the stairs. After a few minutes passed, Lady came out in a t-shirt and sat down next to me.

"We didn't mean to upset you. I thought you were okay with this. What happened?" she asked me, in the voice of an angel that just so happened to be filled with the spooge of the devil.

"I'm sorry, it's fine. I just wasn't expecting it is all," I explained.

The next night the three of us headed out to a hotel. Pepe had reserved a room with a hot tub. We drank gallons of alcohol and soaked in the tub, naked. Soon, I was ready to let my guard down. The three of us climbed onto the bed.

First, I made out with Pepe. Then, Lady made out with me. Next, they made out with each other. Lady started sucking on Pepe's man part while I stuck a vibrator up Lady's who-ha.

Lady did not like this, she only liked clitoral action. This was the night I learned all women are not made equal. I may be an amazing lay in bed with a man but when it comes to a woman, I'm clueless.

No matter, Pepe was coming in for the kill. He was going to take over. That's when it happened, the plane crashed. The building imploded. Pepe went soft. He started to freak out because he had failed as a man.

Pepe was a little crazy. Instead of maybe trying some deep breathing exercises or perhaps taking a cigarette break, he broke beer bottles before smashing his head into the wall. He was enraged at himself and his ruined performance and continued to destroy the hotel room for several minutes.

Lady, being heaven-sent (or perhaps just prepared after being in a relationship with Pepe for seven years) worked her charm and calmed the psychopath down.

The three of us were all sitting on the bed together when I noticed it for the first time.

Genital wart.

That's right, Pepe had HPV. He had a huge wart on the side of his member. Lady noticed me looking at it.

"That's not what you think it is," she explained, "Pepe zipped himself up a few years ago and it scarred."

I was 21, I was entranced with Lady. Although, I was skeptical at first, I believed her.

A few nights later, Lady went out of town for the weekend to visit family. Pepe and I decided to spend the weekend at the pool. We smoked cigarettes and guzzled energy drinks mixed with malt liquor, we were drunk and wired. We didn't sleep for days. Literally, we sat at the pool for 36 hours straight. When we began, it was daytime, then it turned into night. The sun came back up again. We looked like Las Vegas Raisins, burned and pruney.

I was in a little, sheer blue-sequined bikini that was actually a burlesque outfit. Basically, it was see-through dental floss. Had I been in any other town I would have been arrested for indecent exposure.

When we finally left the pool that second evening, we went back to the apartment and had sex for the first time. Pepe fell in love.

Lady arrived home the next day and Pepe told Lady that he wanted to marry me. As expected, Lady was devastated, I was too. Actually, I liked Lady more than Pepe, but I was stuck and had nowhere to go. I was young and dumb.

Lady moved out of state and back home with her family a few days later.

My adventures with Pepe were just beginning.

I talked to Lady about a year after everything had happened. She told me that she had met someone and that they had moved in together. Lady was pregnant. This was exciting news for her because she loved children. She had wanted a baby for a long time but Pepe had refused to give her one.

I teased her and told her she was stupid. Why would she want a kid? I was twenty one and my biological clock had not yet started ticking. Lady was patient with me in her explanation and I decided I was happy for her after all.

A week later, at only four months along, Lady went into labor. The doctors were unable to save her baby. Lady was diagnosed with cervical cancer. As it turns out, because of Pepe's zipper lie, Lady never had herself tested for HPV. She can no longer have children.

Dead Brothers Are No Fun At All

I was eleven when my little brother died. Living in California with my grandparents at the time, my grandfather called me in from playing outside and told me that we were going to Las Vegas in an hour to be with my family. He instructed me to go upstairs, take a bath and put on my pajamas because it would be dark by the time we arrived at my parent's house.

I remember asking him why we were making such a sudden trip. With tears in his eyes, he said to me, "Your brother just had a heart attack. He died."

I was in complete shock.

At eleven years old, I had never lost anyone to death before. All of my grandparents and great-grandparents were still living. I had flushed a fish or two in my lifetime, but that was an entirely different thing.

I remember floating up the stairs, as if I was in a bad dream, and into the bathroom. Once I entered, I shut the door behind me, fell back against it and slid down to the floor. Then came the flooding of tears.

It's amazing how shocking news like this can be, especially when you have been waiting for it your entire life. You see, my brother was born ill. He had a terminal heart disease called, Tetrology of Fallot. His first of many open heart surgeries occurred when he was only a week old, he was never expected to live to begin with.

Nobody could say for sure why he was born this way. It could have been bad luck, genetics, or perhaps my mother's recreational drug use.

My mom disclosed that little secret to me like she did most everything, after drinking way too much wine when I was far too young to understand. I still remember "the birds and the bees" talk at age five. I was just starting kindergarten, "The boy puts his weenie inside you. It gets big and hard! It feels good to boys. You are a girl so you probably won't like it," my mom explained to me while laughing.

"You are lucky I am telling you this stuff. My mother never told me, I had to find out from my classmates when I was in high school. Boy was that embarrassing!"

The next day I remember wandering into kindergarten, I had to sit next to a male student. I was terrified of him and all boys for that matter. They needed to keep their things in their pants and far away from me. You know, pretty much the opposite of how I am now.

If you ask my mother about this, she will tell you I'm lying. She, too, suffers from an ongoing medical condition, alcohol-induced memory loss.

I don't remember much of that drive through the desert, or anything before I walked into the hospital room for the first time. My brother was in a coma. He was lying in bed with his chest bloodied and stitched closed. The stitches were over the numerous scars he already had on his chest from his uncountable previous surgeries. Tubes were coming out of his mouth and nose. They were connected to beeping machines. He was bone thin and ghost white.

The paramedics had miraculously revived my brother. Between my dad's CPR and the medical defibrillation, my brother's body was brought back to life after being dead for over five minutes.

He was breathing with the help of a machine. Emergency surgery had mended his heart for now but would his brain ever be able to recover? We waited the entire summer to find out.

After spending some time in the hospital with my little brother, my grandparents took me and my youngest brother, Gooey, back to my parent's house for some rest. I was still awake in bed when my dad came home from the hospital that night.

My dad and I sat in the kitchen alone while the rest of the house slept. He made us both turkey sandwiches and we ate them together in the dimly lit room. While digesting our midnight snacks, he told me his version of what had happened that day.

Sunday morning my parents woke up and my dad made his usual weekend brunch of potatoes, eggs and toast. While they were cooking, my brothers played in the front of the apartment, on the lawn. As another part of their Sunday morning tradition, my parents enjoyed a few bloody mary's. Once those were gone, they moved on to mimosas. After finishing a few bottles of cheap champagne, they were trashed and sleepy and decided to take a nap or more likely, pass out.

My brothers, ages seven and two, continued to play outside alone, unsupervised in the Las Vegas heat. After an hour or so, my mom awoke completely dehydrated and needing water. She got up and stumbled, still intoxicated, into the kitchen. On her way to the sink, she heard a strange moaning sound by the front door. Curious and needing to check on the kids anyway, she opened it.

That's when she saw it. My little brother was lying on the porch, dead.

Frantic, my mom screamed for my dad to wake up while running for the phone. My dad got up and immediately started performing CPR on my little brother. Gooey stood there helplessly, not understanding what was going on.

Within minutes, the paramedics arrived and shocked my brother with paddles from the portable defibrillating machine. After several attempts they were able to recover a heartbeat.

Swarms of nosy neighbors gathered around to watch the show. My mother climbed into the ambulance with my brother and they were rushed to the hospital.

It was a horrible feeling waking up in that apartment the next morning not knowing the fate of my brother. I tried to focus my attention on my baby brother instead. I took Gooey outside with me to get some air and play a little bit before returning to the hospital. That's when it happened.

I was greeted by nosy neighbor number one, "Is your brother OK?" he wanted to know.

"I'm not sure yet," I answered.

"Why not? It's not like it's a big deal!" he stammered.

"Excuse me?" I asked in shock, "My brother is in a coma! The doctors think he may be brain dead!"

"Wow! Just from choking on a chicken bone? That's crazy! I think your brother may have been brain dead to start with."

What the hell?

Just then, nosy neighbors number two and three walked up. Number two started to speak, "Hey, *****. What is going on with your brother? I heard he hit his head pretty good falling out of that old tree," she pointed to the tree in front of my apartment.

"He didn't fall out of a tree!" I corrected her.

Nosy neighbor one chimed in, "Where did you hear that he fell? He didn't fall! He choked on a chicken bone!"

More people began to join us. Quickly, I was becoming a ghetto celebrity. I did not like this.

I was trying to deal with the situation as best I could at eleven years old while still comforting my baby brother. These people were acting like the damn paparazzi.

"Listen," I finally shouted, "My brother had a heart attack. He is in a coma. The doctors don't know if he will ever recover."

Another neighbor walked up, "A heart attack? No, that's not what I heard! I heard he choked on a chicken bone and then fell out of that tree."

I had been standing there long enough. I grabbed Gooey and went inside.

My brother eventually made it out of the coma. His brain function returned to normal. However, he has no memory of the incident or any part of his life before it happened, nor does he remember that entire summer of recovery.

A little while after this all happened, I told him that alcohol induced memory loss must be genetic. He told me to fuck off.

Bob Light Betty
&
The Mullet Man

The first alcohol I ever gave up was gin and I will tell you why. It all happened one shitty Saturday night in the ghetto of Long Beach. I was picked up by my favorite ginger, Red. We headed out to go bar hopping fairly, early in the evening since we had a few stops to make.

My drink of choice that evening was gin and tonic. I had probably twelve or maybe fifteen of them that night, I was an alcoholic.

Our first stop, bar number one. Red parked and we walked inside. Sitting at the bar was our mutual friend, Betty. That's a lie. Betty was not sitting at the bar, she was passed out cold on the bar. Her head rested in a puddle of her own drool. Red and I behaved as any caring and responsible friends would after finding themselves in such a situation. We bought ourselves drinks, laughed and toasted to Betty.

Eventually, we drove her home.

While on our way to unload our loaded friend, a car cut us off. Red slammed on the brakes. That's when we heard it.

CLUNK! CLUNK! CLUNK!

Then, something hard slammed into my ankle, "Owe! Fuck!" I screamed.

"What the hell was that?" Red asked me.

I peered under my seat and found several unopened cans of cheap beer rolling around freely. I looked back at Betty, she was still asleep but her purse had tipped over, the contents strewn on the floor of the back seat. That bitch had snuck a damn case of Bob Light into the bar.

After dragging Betty inside her apartment we headed off to bar number two. Once inside, I started ordering my gin and tonics. Our plans having been delayed by our mission of mercy, I was downing them pretty fast.

Two white trash men in dirty shirts and mullet haircuts (they had probably been wearing both since the 1980's) approached us and challenged us to a game of bar pool.

"Sure, we'll play, if you buy us drinks first, Bubba," I drunkenly slurred.

"What are we playing for, your trailer?" Red added.

"How about you let us take turns kicking your dog around?" I asked.

"Nice wife beater, did you get it on sale at the Salvation Army last weekend?" Red taunted.

That is where my memory ended.

The next day, I awoke to a knock on my door. It was Red. I dragged my naked, half-dead ass out of bed, wrapped a towel haphazardly around myself and let her in. She had a bag of rum, mint, lime....she was making mojitos!

Damn, do I love that ginger bitch!

"I'm glad to see you made it home! I was worried about you!" Red said, as she handed me my bra.

I gave her a confused look. She started laughing hysterically.

"What? Why are you laughing?"

"I see that you have met your new neighbors, I just introduced myself them," Red said.

"No, I haven't met them, yet," I responded.

Red grabbed her gut before bending over in laughter.

"What? What's so funny?"

She handed me a mojito, "Oh, my God," she gasped. Red literally laughed until mojito was running out of her freckled nose.

Then, she finally told me the story.

We had lost our game of pool to the toothless truckers the night before. As payment, one of them wanted a kiss from me. So, I did what any drunken skank would do. I made out with a mullet man for an hour.

Finally, after she was thoroughly repulsed, Red dragged me out of the bar and drove me home. At least, she tried. We were roughly three blocks away from my apartment when it happened.

Stopped at a red light, I jumped out of Red's car and ran down an alley. Red tried to snag me as I bolted out of her car, but failed. She drove around half the night looking for me to no avail.

Skipping, I had passed through the alley and crossed onto a major intersection. There, I removed my shirt and flung it. Passing down yet another block, I removed my skirt and dropped it. As I rounded my street, I shot my panties from my hand like a rubber band. I made it to my front porch and in front of my new neighbors, took off my bra, before falling up my stairs completely naked, dumping out the contents of my purse.

The two little Asian girls, whom had just moved in below me, watched this in complete shock. One of them asked me if I was okay.

That's when I did it. In my drunken state, I stood up, grabbed my empty purse and threw it at her. Then I screamed, "Come on bitch! Let's go! I'll kick your yellow ass!"

Now, this was Long Beach after all. As it turns out the sisters were drinking too. One of the girls lunged towards me ready to attack.

Lucky for me, her sister grabbed her and pulled her inside just in time to save my sloshed, stupid ass.

I eventually made it up to my own apartment and passed out.

The girls were outside that morning when Red arrived. They gleefully told her the story.

I ended up gifting them a bottle of hard liquor not long after that as an apology along with a hair service. We all became great friends.

Mullet guy called and left me several messages for a good week after our spit exchange. I don't remember giving him my number. Nor do I remember him removing his teeth prior to kissing me as Red mentioned a little while later. I'm pretty happy that I didn't catch mono. I never drank gin again.

Red still talks about this. Right now she is laughing.

Bitch.

Coke Who Res

I have two "besties" that I have known since we went to junior high school together in Las Vegas, Laverne and Tangerae'. We call each other "Who Res." It all started from a broken up, drunken text I sent them when I was living in California. I meant to call them whores.

Like I said, I was drunk, I mistyped, I spelled it out in two words: Who. Res. They were so drunk they read it in two. I seriously think it took those dumb bitches a good week to figure out what I had called them.

The three of us have created much trouble together. The apple didn't fall far from the tree. Within thirty minutes of her arrival from Texas, Shirley almost got the four of us arrested. Shirley is Laverne's mother.

Tangerae', Laverne and I started that fateful day at my house having wine and pigging out on pizza. I was very large back then, I ate a lot of pizza. Also, cheese puffs.

As the sun set, the three of us piled into Laverne's car and headed to the airport, to pick up Shirley. We parked in the lot and then made our way to the terminal. Once inside we took a seat on a bench and waited.

Laverne received a text from Shirley not long after, she was off the plane and headed our way. We started walking in Shirley's direction. That's when we saw it.

Shirley was on the floor. She was on her back, kicking her legs in the air. Her skirt had fallen down exposing her granny panties and the non-groomed, gray surroundings. Uh huh, that old bag was laughing like a hyena on nitrous oxide. Shirley was drunk. Yippee!

Wanting to avoid a run in with TSA, we helped Shirley up and got her to the car quickly. Well, as quickly as we could. Shirley kept stumbling.

Once inside, we buckled her up and headed out to the casino. This was Las Vegas after all! We were going to gamble. The night was still young.

On our way to the casino, Shirley started talking about the cocaine her son had smuggled in from Mexico. She told us it was the purest shit she ever snorted. Laverne started to pout.

"Why didn't you bring any for me?" she whined.

Sure as shit, Shirley reached down and pulled off her mammoth, sheet-like, cunt covers.

"I did!" she exclaimed, "In my panties!"

There, between two maxi pads was a bag of rock cocaine. Genius!

We pulled into the parking garage of the casino and Laverne parked her car. Though, we didn't know it yet, Laverne had settled us right under a surveillance camera.

Shirley handed her poody powder over to Laverne. Laverne began cutting up lines. Then, with a rolled up twenty, both began snorting.

"What does that smell like, Laverne?" I chuckled, "Are you enjoying the smell of your mom's cooch?"

"Shut up, Who Res!"

The duo then offered some to Tangerae' and me.

There was a time in my life that I loved cocaine but that time had long since expired.

"No thanks, I'm not in the mood to sniff cat tonight," I said.

Tangerae' declined as well. She and I were anxious to get into the casino. Laverne and Shirley were having too much fun and taking too long. After about ten minutes, we persuaded them out of the car. The four of us headed towards the elevator. We didn't make it.

"Stop right there!" it was a security guard on a bike, "I just got a call that one of you ladies was seen putting a foreign substance up your nose."

Without skipping a beat, wasted and fluttering, Shirley said, "Yes, sir. I was using my nasal allergy medication. I just got off the plane from Texas, I always have problems in the dry climate. Here's my plane ticket."

Shirley had obviously done this before. Though the guard was skeptical, after a few minutes of interrogation, he let us go.

We gambled all our money away in a half-hour, which was good because I could not enjoy myself after that. My OCPD had kicked in. I kept looking over my shoulder for the police, waiting for them to haul our stupid asses off to jail.

After a few drinks and a few wasted twenties, we made our way back to the car. Laverne dropped me at my house and I said my goodbyes.

Then, just as they were about to pull away I had a change of heart.
That's right, I stopped them. I walked over to the passenger window. Shirley rolled it down.
"Give me a line," I said.
That white nosed, corpse of a skank did. I snorted that dried up, vaginal discharge scented powder right up my nose.

It smelled like drugs.

Rockabilly's Are Stupid

I was twenty one years old when I began my relationship with Pepe. Lady had packed up most of her and Pepe's apartment before moving back to her home state to be with her family. That left Pepe and me alone in Las Vegas with really no way to support ourselves. Pepe was a pure bred douche bag. At thirty six, he was pulling in minimum wage working retail at the local music store.

Lady had been supporting them both through stripping, I had also been stripping, well attempting. Like I implied already, I was the worst stripper there ever was, and I didn't make any money.

Being low on options, Pepe called his brother in Tucson and asked if we could stay there for a little while, until we got on our feet. His brother, Tim, agreed.

Pepe's brother was a rockabilly who had just gotten out of prison. He had a three bedroom house. Though all the rooms were rented out, he told us we could stay in the "tiki lounge." The lounge was just an additional room built on the side of the house. It did not have AC and was extremely hot. However, it did possess a tiny black and white TV, a little keepsake from Tim's prison cell.

Tim liked to joke, "I used to watch Startha Mewart on that TV when I was in prison. Guess who is in there now?"

Also living in the house was Tim's "unpleasantly plump" girlfriend, Angela. I lovingly referred to her as "Anger-la."

Anger-la was the biggest, fattest bitch that ever lived. She had an obsession with cleaning that included dusting plants. Everyday you could find her in the living room with a dry cloth and a ficus. This was very confusing, especially considering the smashed gecko corpse that lived between the front door and it's frame. She had never bothered to remove that.

Anger-la loved to shop online for accessories. She would only buy things if they had "rockabilly fashion" written in their description.

Another endearing quality, Anger-la had the most annoying nasally voice ever. You could hear it echo through the yard when she fucked Tim, "AAA-HHHH-AAA!"

I would spill things on the carpet intentionally, just to piss her off. Sometimes, in the mornings, I would hide her plants. You could hear her stampede through the house, like an elephant in heat, looking for each plant. This brought me much joy.

Also in the house were Tim's two roommates, Joe and Bobby. Bobby was a nice guy and he kept to himself for the most part. There was just one thing strange about Bobby (besides him being a pansy rockabilly), he kept three rather large hissing cockroaches as pets. He would walk around the house with them on his shirt, petting them.

Very disgusting.

Immediately upon arrival, I went looking for a job. I was hired pretty quickly at a sports lounge as a server. Remember how I said I was the worst stripper that ever lived? I'm also probably the worst waitress. It only took two weeks before I was fired.

My main concern was not holding down a job back then, anyway. It was attaining and consuming alcohol. I always had plenty of hooch. This was a good thing because my relationship with Pepe was not. Pepe was very jealous. Anytime he thought a man was looking at me he would start a confrontation.

One extremely hot, Tucson morning after having gotten fired from my job, I woke up next to Pepe, from a tickling sensation.

"Stop it, Pepe!" I giggled, "It's too early for that," I said while slapping his hand, only it wasn't his hand that I hit. It made a slight crackling sound.

What the hell was that? I opened my eyes and looked at my shoulder. That's when I saw it. Them.

I screamed louder than a slut in a basketball team's locker room.

That's right, I jumped up and did a dance like an Indian in a rain ceremony.

We were covered in cockroaches. Hissing cockroaches. I told you rockabilly's suck! One of Bobby's pets had bred. It had several thousand babies. They had escaped.

After this, I needed a drink, even if it was only eight o'clock in the morning. Pepe and I didn't stop drinking all day. We consumed all the liquor we had and were without income to purchase more.

Luckily, that night we were invited to party. The beer was everywhere. I devised what I thought to be a brilliant plan, one beer for me, one for my purse. Once my purse became too heavy to carry, I made a trip to my car and emptied it into the trunk. Repeat.

Tim caught wind of this and flipped out. He called me lots of unpleasant names. Pepe decided, instead of sticking up for me to his little brother, that he would take me home. I said goodbye to my new male acquaintance that I had been talking to and we were off.

"Who the fuck was that guy you were talking to?" Pepe wanted to know.

"His name is Daryl. He is a gay and he owns a hair salon," I said, "He told me to come see him after I take my cosmetology licensing exam out here next month and he will give me a job."

WHAP!

Pepe hit me with the back of his hand, right across my beautiful face.

"You fucking stupid, lying bitch!" he screamed, "That guy wasn't a faggot! He had his nuts all over you!" Pepe's eyes were bloodshot and twitching.

I didn't respond, I was in shock. Silently, I kept my eyes glued to the road.

We pulled up to the house, Pepe continued his rant, "You stupid, fucking whore!"

I got out of the car and started walking towards the lounge, I opened the back gate.

"I'm talking to you! Look at me you stupid bitch!" he continued.

That was enough, Pepe was going down. I turned around, made a fist and socked Pepe in the side of his ugly, acne scarred head. Puss shot out.

"Asshole!" I screamed.

Pepe did not like this. Before I knew what was happening next, he pushed me onto the ground. I landed on my back with a "thud." He sat on top of me and again started slapping me in the face.

"You like this, Bitch?" he yelled, "Look what you are making me do to you!"

I squirmed but it was no use, his knees were already holding down my arms.

WACK!

Pepe continued to slap me. I tried to spit on him but the liquid just came right back down and landed onto my own face. Crying, I was attempting to kick him, but my feet were not even coming close to making contact with any part of his body.

Just then, Tim walked up. I was saved!

"Keep it down!" Tim yelled, "One of the neighbors might call the cops! One call and I go back to prison!"

With that, Tim disappeared into the house. I was not saved. Tim didn't even care.

Pepe eventually let me go, but not until he made me apologize. I walked into our room, gathered my things and took off in my car. It was three in the morning and I was broke.

I sat in front of a grocery store down the street until it opened. Then, I called my grandfather and asked him to wire me enough money to make the drive back to Los Angeles.

I didn't see Pepe again for six months, but that's another story.

Big Dick Mick:
An Understatement

I remember the months that followed the first Donut dumping. Desperately, I tried to forget about him. In one of my attempts, I posted a personal ad online looking for a date. Included were several drunken, slutty pictures of myself. Within the first twenty four hours, I had received over a hundred responses.

Red came by early one evening to help me sort through them. Her favorite was a twenty-something hunk with a shaved head. In his picture, he was holding a flower. I found out later that he had cropped his ex-girlfriend out.

Like the desperate, drunken, heartbroken whore I was, I responded to Mick, along with thirty five others.

"You are alright looking, plus you like flowers. I will consider a date with you," I wrote.

Mick responded, "I will see you at six on Saturday and I will bring you flowers."

DING DONG!

My doorbell rang. Mick was right on time that evening and he had flowers as promised. I love flowers.

He drove us downtown to a restaurant where we ate sushi and drank martinis. After our meal, I invited Mick back to my place. Okay, my grandma's place. We drank more, laughed and snacked on some leftover corned beef and cabbage I had in the fridge. The leftover cabbage was soggy and disgusting. I decided to throw it off the balcony and into the neighbor's yard.

Mick liked this. He thought my antics were hilarious. I thought Mick was okay.

In retrospect, Mick was by far the best guy I had ever dated. He was strikingly handsome, nice, ambitious and funnier than shit. Also, there was one more redeeming quality Mick possessed.

I grabbed Mick by his bulbous bald head that night and threw him onto my bed. After a few minutes of spit swapping, he helped me out of my panties. Then, he entered me.

Literally, I thought I would break in half. I had never felt anything so gigantic and hard in my life. It felt like he was trying to fist me. This guy could put a beer can to shame.

Big Dick Mick, total understatement. His schlong looked like it belonged to a rhinoceros or perhaps a dinosaur. Of course, I was still obsessed with Donut. So, I couldn't be bothered to notice that Mick was a catch. This was fine by Mick because I was too much of a drunk for him to take me seriously anyway.

I decided that Mick would do for the time being. My friends all encouraged this, they loved Mick. Saturday quickly became our date night.

Mick would come by in the evening, either I would make him dinner or we would go out. We would get drunk and have bone rearranging sex. The next morning, we would meet my friends for brunch.

Our relationship was simple, we never had any talks about where it was or wasn't going. We never had any fights. There were no expectations.

Mick and I also shared the same sick sense of humor. It became tradition that once a week I would mail him a blank card with a baby on the front, purchased at the dollar store. Inside, I would inscribe a new dead baby joke.

Mick enjoyed this, as did I, immensely. I have always been the queen of inappropriate happenings. Remember that picture Bahssten took of me pissing near the dumpster, outside of MME Smack Down? Well, once she had it developed, I signed it, framed it and gifted it to Mick.

One weekend, after several months of dating, Mick didn't come by. He had met another girl who wasn't a drunk. She possessed a better body than I had. I know because he showed me a picture of her naked ass.

Whatever, I didn't really care. It's not like he was Donut, anyway. I was still dreaming of my sweet glazed, honey roll. I started hanging out with Mackey, an old acquaintance, instead. If by hanging out I mean humping.

One afternoon, several weeks later, Mick called me up. His new girl had dumped him for her ex. Not long after, he had broken his leg. Mick was helpless, he couldn't drive his car. Also, he had errands to run and he was lonely. Aww, he needed my help.

Considering that I'm a low-self-esteemed slut, I helped out my pal. Of course I did, I made and brought him over dinner and a pie before carting his gimp ass around town.

A little while after, I discovered that I was pregnant. Mackey had knocked me up. Guess what, just around the same time, Mick found out his ex was pregnant too, with his baby.

Twinsies!

Just as Mackey decided he wanted nothing to do with my pregnancy, Mick's ex told him she didn't want him to have anything to do with hers.

The two of us, sad, lonely and pathetic, started sleeping together again.

One evening, roughly five months into my pregnancy, huge as a house, there was a knock on the balcony door adjacent to my bedroom. I rolled my bloated, beastly body out of bed.

That's when I heard it, singing. What the hell? With my pulse racing I opened the curtains.

Standing there, on my balcony, was my drunken, coke-can-cocked Romeo. Mick had decided to climb up to my room instead of knocking on the front door. He was toasted. This brought me much amusement.

I let the crotch crocodile, and its host, inside my room. Mick laid me down on my bed, lifted my skirt and stuffed his third leg into my hot, skank trap. Mick, in his own words, was "sword fighting" my unborn child.

The next day we had brunch with my friend, Bahssten, before heading out to the beach together. Bahssten and Mick had obvious chemistry. You couldn't ignore it. I decided, since I was already knocked up and no longer dating material, that I would step back and give the two of them my blessings.

The morning of my baby shower Bahssten called me up. She was at Mick's, she had stayed the night with him for the first time. I did not like this and I flipped out. That's right, I was hormonal and enraged for no reason at all.

First, I uninvited them both to my baby shower. Then, I re-invited Bahssten. Poor thing, she came anyway and felt guilty the entire time.

I made all my friends be really mean to her.

As it turned out, Bahssten and Mick were not a perfect. They ended up hating each other. Bahssten told Mick he was stupid and that he could never succeed in law school like she could.

Mick proved her wrong, he is now an attorney. He ended up marrying the girl with the hot ass. Their son is the same age as mine.

I found Mick on an internet site a few months ago and messaged him a dead baby joke. Not surprisingly, much like most of the men I have dated in the past, Mick ignored me.

Hey, Mick! If you happen to read this:
Q: How are babies and the elderly alike?
A: Both are fun to throw out of moving vehicles.

How I Lost My Virginity, Twice

I was fifteen and I just wanted to get it over with already. Being a teenage sociopath and seeking experience, I slept with the first idiot who came along. That's right, to lose my virginity.

His name was Mason Hudge, but I like to refer to him as Mason Huge. I will tell you why.

Huge was in the same grade as I was. Unlike me, he was into the heavy metal scene. Accordingly, he wore all black, combat boots and a spiked collar. He didn't have much of a personality and was really short. Also, I'm pretty sure Huge thought he was a vampire.

After making out with half the neighborhood my freshman year and being called a tease, I decided I was finally ready to see what all the fuss was about. That and I was hanging out with my new friend, Butterfly, who was the biggest slut that ever lived.

"*****, I can't believe you are still a virgin! I've slept with eighteen people and I'm younger than you. Sex is amazing, you have to try it."

"Okay, Butterfly, but with who?"

"Don't you have a crush on anyone?"

"Well, there is this guy in my math class who is kinda' cute."

"Do it with him!"

Thought activated.

The next day I was sitting in my math class when Huge approached me. I can't even remember what stupid thing he said to me but I cut to the chase pretty quickly.

"Huge, what are you doing after school this week? We should hang out."

"My parents will be gone on Wednesday, do you want to come over. I might be able to get us a few beers."

"Wednesday is fine, I'll walk home with you," I said.

That next Wednesday, I followed my little death rock munchkin home and into his room.

Huge pointed to my studded bracelet, "That's really cool. Can I borrow it?"

"Uh, I guess," I said, taking it off and handing it to him.

My metallic man grabbed me by the hair and pulled me onto his bed. We started making out. Then that little fucker bit me! I don't mean a love bite either, this guy laid into me like I was a juicy steak. He didn't stop until he drew blood.

I wanted to scream out in pain but I didn't want him to think I was a wimp. Plus, I really wanted to get the sex thing over with. So, I pulled off his pants.

"Are you okay with this?" he asked me.

I nodded without looking down, without looking anywhere near his wooden stake for that matter. He reached into his drawer and pulled out a condom while I hid under the blankets with my eyes closed until he was done putting it on.

Next, he rolled on top of me. I could feel him fumbling with something down there but I wasn't sure what he was doing. He bit me again while rocking back and forth on top of me for about thirty seconds.

That was it. Huge got up and started getting dressed, "My mom will be home in about fifteen minutes so you should probably go."

I was really confused, but I put my clothes back on. Huge walked me to his front door.

"Can I have my bracelet back now?" I asked.

"I'll give it you in school tomorrow," he answered before shutting his door in my face.

I started my hour long trek home on foot. As I was finding my way through the darkening ghetto, I reflected on what had just happened. Finally, I had lost my virginity. I had sex and I didn't even feel it. Something must be terribly wrong with me or maybe I had the loosest vagina ever. Could it be that I didn't have any nerves down there? That couldn't be the case because I could feel it when I peed. Sometimes it even hurt when I inserted tampons but I had just had sex and felt nothing. What could this mean?

Finally, I decided I needed to ask all my friends. The very next day I did just that.

"*****, you had sex but didn't feel it? What did it look like? Was it big?"

"I didn't look at it, I was too scared!"

Everyone pretty much came to the same conclusion, Huge must have not been huge after all. He must have been very small.

Several weeks passed and I had pretty much forgotten all about this. I wasn't speaking to Huge because he never did bring me back my bracelet.

I was hanging out at the park with a group of my friends when it happened.

I was introduced to an angel, his name was Leo and he was beautiful. As it turned out, Leo lived a state away with his mom but spent every other weekend in town visiting his dad. His dad lived just a few blocks from me.

Leo and I clicked right away. We spent that entire weekend together. I was sad when Leo left but couldn't wait for his return.

Two interminable weeks later Leo was back. I had fantasized about him the entire time he was gone. My mind had been made up, I was going let him penetrate me as soon as he returned. That day I knocked on his dad's apartment door around eight in the morning. Leo had gone out of his way to make sure his dad bought me a bottle of two dollar, strawberry flavored wine (the drink of choice for any fifteen year old girl) before leaving for work that morning.

Awww, how sweet, Leo thought he had to liquor me up first. He didn't know that I wasn't planning on being a challenge. I sipped on my headache juice and made out with my sexy, seven inch Godsend.

After about forty five minutes, Leo invited me into his father's bed. I laid back and whispered softly to him, "Do you have a condom?"

"Oh! You want to…I mean… YEAH! Right here, hang on!"

Leo slipped on his penis cover before slipping inside of me. What I felt next I was not expecting. I was being forced open by something big and strong. It was very awkward.

Hooray!

Hiding my shock, I made some moaning sounds because TV had taught me I was supposed to. I tried to wiggle my hips to his rhythm but I had no clue what I was doing or feeling.

I WAS DEFINITELY FEELING SOMETHING!

When it was all over, Leo rolled to the other side of the bed and looked at me.

"Are you on your period?" he shyly asked.

"No."

"Wait, were you a virgin?" he almost yelled in shock.

I stared over at him blankly.

Leo jumped up, "Why didn't you tell me?"

I just shrugged.

What was I going to tell him? I didn't even know I was still a virgin. Pffft, I was just glad that I had felt it.

I continued to date Leo for another visit or two. You know, until he boinked Butterfly, but that's another story.

CarniHELL: The Cruise

RING! RING! RING!

I rolled my hung-over ass out of bed and looked at the clock. It was just after nine on a Sunday morning. Whoever was calling me, it had better be important.

"Hello?" I barely crackled the word out of my Mojave Desert conditioned mouth.

"It's Mom. Listen, the whole family is going on a cruise to Mexico next month. I'm booking the trip right now, do you want to go?"

"Huh?"

"What's wrong with you? You sound drunk! Are you drunk at nine in the morning? Oh, my God!"

I sighed in exasperation, "No, I was drunk last night. I just woke up, it's early!"

"You are so lazy. Are you going or not? I need to book it now."

"Yeah, I guess so."

"Okay, your ticket is a hundred and fifty dollars. Mail me a check today."

"Whoa! Whoa, no, I'm broke. Never mind. You have a good trip. I gotta' go."

I rolled my fat ass over and covered my head with a blanket. That bitch just woke me up for nothing. This reminded me of the time she had given me a microwave as a house warming present and then insisted I pay her forty bucks for it.

A week later, it happened. I was roughly three bottles into my usual case of night-cap when my phone rang. It was HER.

"Listen, I talked to Squirrel (her husband) and he said we could buy your cruise ticket as a birthday gift for you if you still wanted to go."

This may very well be how I became such a good negotiator.

"Yeah, cool, I'll go."

"Okay, you will be sharing a room with your brother, Gooey."

The night before the cruise, I carefully packed my bag. I placed six bottles of red wine and two bottles of vodka inside. Then, with the space I could find left over, I shoved in whatever clothes would fit around the bottles. That night I went to sleep excited about my wondrous weekend on the high seas.

By six o'clock that morning, I was up and out of my apartment. I drove down to the nearby port and found my family. My luggage was really heavy and without wheels, my hands were starting to blister from the weight before we even boarded the vessel. Carefully hiding my grimaces, I followed everyone through the line and up to the boat entrance.

Yippee!

They were taking family photos. Forcibly, I assumed the position.

After the photos, the staff handed out our room keys. They asked if we wanted our luggage delivered. Although my hand was almost bleeding at this point, I wasn't about to let go of my hooch. Gooey and I marched the four miles to our room, leaving the rest of the family with promises to meet at the group safety demonstration before the boat left port.

The interior of the boat was a joke. It looked like 1950's Las Vegas threw up, riddled with little "Tijuana type" touches. It even smelled that way, too. Like shit.

Gooey and I entered the only working glass elevator after waiting in line for twenty minutes. We descended slowly down to the darkened dungeon of our discounted room accommodations.

I opened the door and we both peered suspiciously into our hat box. I am not exaggerating, I have spent time in jail cells with roomier floor plans than this. The beds were tiny with one inch thick plastic mattresses suspended from the ceiling. I'm pretty sure my ass was wider than the entire bed. In the corner of the room was a minuet, mounted TV. It had one channel and played the same movie (over and over and over) the entire weekend.

The en-suite bathroom was so small that the door could only open partway before hitting the miniature sink. My head touched the ceiling while I took a dump. The shower head descended over the toilet.

Shrugging, I walked over to the only window to at least get a look at the ocean view. Pulling open the curtain instead revealed more of the wall. That's right, a curtain over a wall. The window was a trick!

We were in CarniHELL!

I needed a drink, good thing that I had packed a lot of wine. As I was pouring myself a cocktail to calm my nerves, a voice began bellowing through the loud-speaker.

"Everyone, please meet in your designated group area in five minutes. We will be going over the safety instructions. Each bed has a life vest secured beneath it. Make sure to bring yours."

I plopped my fat ass down on my yoga mat of a bed and sipped my delicious grape poison. Gooey was frantically looking for his life vest.

"Gooey, what are you doing? Sit down and relax, let's watch a movie."

"I need my vest! We only have five minutes to meet with the group."

"Calm down, Gooey. We aren't meeting with the group. That's a stupid idea."

"What? We need to know the safety precautions, what if something happens?" Gooey was startled.

"Listen, we are on a stupid cruise ship. There is another boat riding directly beside to us. If anything were to happen we could just swim over to it. We aren't even a mile from the coast. It's a joke, Gooey. Seriously, have you ever heard of a cruise ship accident (this was back in 2003 before captains became drunk idiots)?"

Gooey thought for a moment, then decided I had a point. He sat down, shut his trap and watched the movie. We could feel the boat set off. I could feel my stomach start to turn.

Once the movie ended and I finished my first bottle of wine, we decided to head out to dinner. There we ran into the rest of our lame family. Lining up like hungry sheep, we stood docilely in line to fill our fat faces. Gooey helped himself to a chocolate soft serve ice cream cone. When he finished that, he took another. Gooey ate those stupid cones as fast as I drank my cheap wine.

It didn't take long for the family trip to get boring.

"Let's go to the casino," I suggested. Gooey could not go because he was only fifteen at the time. Instead, he headed to the arcade.

Once I reached the casino, I was surprised to find that it was closed. Uh huh, the casino was only open when in Mexican waters, and that would not be until the following afternoon. I looked inside to find that there was not much to it. Six slot machines and a tiny blackjack table.

Stupid.

I headed to the arcade to find Gooey. He was just standing there against a wall, bored.

"It costs $5 a game here, that's all I brought. My avatar died in ten seconds, these games suck," he complained.

"This whole cruise thing really sucks. How should we try to entertain ourselves now?"

"We could go watch the comedy show," Gooey suggested.

On our way, I refilled my wine pitcher and Gooey grabbed another chocolate cone.

The show lasted forty minutes. It was not funny.

We had only made it to seven o'clock. Gooey and I went back to our room and after watching the same movie three more times, finally fell asleep.

We both awoke several hours later.

"What time is it?" Gooey asked me.

"I don't know, my cell phone doesn't have reception and the screen is doing something weird. Where's the clock?"

"There isn't a clock in the room and I forgot my watch at home."

In a half-asleep daze, I opened the curtains.

DOPE! Stupid wall.

"I'll go to mom's room and see if they have a clock," Gooey offered.

Five minutes later he was back, "Mom is not answering her door. There was not even a clock in the hall, I had to ask a stranger. It is nine twenty in the morning. We docked in

Ensenada twenty minutes ago, I think everyone may already be in the city."

"Those assholes left without us! NOOOOO!"

"Well, we can go look for them," Gooey suggested.

"Are you crazy? I am not going into Mexico alone with you! We could be kidnapped and murdered. This sucks, let's go get some breakfast."

Before heading out I made sure to refill my bucket-o-wine. We made it to the buffet and again loaded our plates with garbage. Well, I loaded my plate with garbage. Gooey loaded his with chocolate soft serve.

After we ate, we decided to hit the pool. It was tiny and filled with screaming children. Also, the water was a suspicious shade of yellow. Instead, we headed over to the hot tub, inside were adults. I reached my foot into the water, only to realize that it was cold.

I started looking around for an employee to complain to and quickly found a generic looking black man in a blue T-shirt who was roughly in his early 30's.

"Excuse me, Sir, the hot tub is cold," I complained.

"It's seventy eight degrees, Ma'am. That's the temperature we keep it at."

"Umm, no, that is not going to work for me. That is the stupidest thing I have ever heard of. You must be joking," I told him.

"No, Ma'am. You sure are pretty. My shift ends in an hour, come find me then and let me buy you a drink."

"What? No."

I turned to Gooey, he had a chocolate mustache, "Let's get out of here."

We wandered around until we found a ping-pong table. Once seated by it, we gave dirty looks to the kids playing until they were spooked enough to leave. Taking it over, we lethargically hit that stupid ball back and forth until the sun went down.

I was so bored that I was contemplating renting a car in Mexico and driving it back to L.A. The only thing stopping me was that damn kidnapping fear. Well, that, and I was poor.

It was getting cold so we headed back to the buffet for dinner. Again, I loaded my plate with deep fried crap while Gooey grabbed his ice cream.

We sat down at a table, the black guy from earlier was seated next to us. He leaned closer to me, "How are you enjoying the cruise so far?"

"It sucks. I want off this stupid boat, already."

"Let me buy you a drink, my shift just ended."

"No, thanks!" I said while rolling my eyes.

After dinner, we decided to explore the outside of the ship. Gooey brought two more chocolate cones along, they were becoming his best friends. I was double fisting myself, with merlot.

It was early December and it was chilly outside.

"I don't really want this last cone, it's too cold. Do you want it?" Gooey asked me.

"No thanks, I'm freezing!"

With that, Gooey threw the damn thing overboard. That same black guy walked up to Gooey, he was STILL following us.

"Excuse me Son, it is illegal to litter into the ocean from a ship. I'll give you a warning this time but don't let me catch you doing it again, okay?"

"No problem, Sir, I'm sorry about that."

The man looked over to me, "Hey, pretty lady. I'm off duty, can I buy you drink?"

"OH MY GOD! NO! I WILL NEVER HAVE A DRINK WITH YOU!"

I grabbed Gooey by the hand and led him back inside.

"Can you believe that guy? He is stalking me. How many times can you tell someone 'no' before they get the hint?"

"Uh, *****, you do know that those were three completely different men that asked you out, right? You have not been talking to the same guy."

"Huh? What? What are you talking about?"

Gooey starting laughing so hard that a crowd of other bored-shitless passengers huddled around us to watch the excitement.

I must be the most unobservant person there ever was.

Just then, a voice started echoing over the intercom loud-speaker, "On behalf of CarniHell, I would like to apologize. I was just informed that we have run out of chocolate soft serve ice cream. This is the first time it has ever happened. Vanilla will still be served along with gelato. Again, I'm sorry for the inconvenience."

My jaw dropped and I pointed at Gooey. Who was the asshole now? I may have been an accidental racist but at least I didn't eat all the ice cream, leaving none for the babies on board.

Gooey was done after that. We walked back to our prison closet and he passed out.

I was still determined to have fun, my efforts were not over. We were not docking back home until the next afternoon and it was still early in the evening.

I was drunk, bored and desperate on the high hell seas, so, I put on a slutty dress and headed out to the night club. Unsurprisingly, it was very disappointing. The club was not much bigger than our bathroom, the music sucked and the men were rude. Well, most of the men, anyway.

"Hello, Beautiful, my name is Roo."

Outstretched a beautiful Aussie arm holding an even more beautiful kamikaze shot. I looked deep into his blue eyes as I downed that shot.

My trip had been saved. Roo and I spent that entire evening together. We danced, we laughed and we went to the midnight comedy show holding hands. It was the same show I had already seen with Gooey, but I didn't mind, Roo was HOT!

After the show, Roo invited me back to his room. It was just down the hall from mine. Once inside, Roo kissed me. Then, I let him pull off my stockings and bend me over his bed. He slid my panties to the side of my ass cheek just before slipping his enormous, left bending joey right inside my pouch.

I moaned, I screamed and I faked an orgasm. Roo filled up the rubber with his man fosters.

After taking a breath, he pulled himself out of me and disposed of the kangaroo skin. Quickly, he slid his pants up, zipped and said to me, "You can leave now."

I stood there for a second, waiting for him to laugh.

He did not.

Stunned, I grabbed my purse and walked to the bedroom door. That is when I felt it, my stockings hit the back of my head. Such a gentleman, that Roo, he didn't want me to forget them.

I cried as I made the walk of shame to my room, alone. Gooey was awake when I entered.

"What the hell happened to you?" he asked me.

After telling him the story, Gooey wanted to kick Roo's ass but I told him to forget about it.

I barely slept at all that night. By six in the morning, I was packed and ready to go. Never in my life had I wanted to touch the ground more. Poor Gooey, I made him get up and wait in line with me. In fear, I hid behind him, hoping not to run into Roo and his friends.

Even though we had docked, the staff would not open the doors to the exit until nine. Those were the longest three hours of my life. My hands literally bled through holding that damn suitcase.

I will never go on another cruise again.

I Make Domestic Violence Funny

After the physical altercation with my boyfriend Pepe that caused me to flee Tucson, I drove back to California crying and bruised. I was returning to live with my grandparents after wasting away my entire summer partying and being an all around twenty one year old idiot. It was time for me to get a normal salon job and settle down.

After a week, I had found the perfect job and I just needed to set some money aside for an apartment. It didn't take long for my loneliness to kick in. Unfortunately, I was pathetic, young and stupid with no self-worth. Out of loneliness, I broke down and called Pepe.

"Hey, Pepe. It's me. How are things going?"

"Holy shit! I didn't think I would hear from you again. You do love me!"

I sighed, "I didn't think I would call but yes, I guess I do."

"Wow. I felt really bad about what happened and I didn't mean to scare you. I won't get that angry again, I just want to be with you."

That was it, I begged my grandparents to let Pepe move in with us while I saved up enough money for the apartment. Eventually they gave in, and I headed off to Tucson to claim my twitchy, eyeliner clad, acne scarred and unstable older man.

Pepe had me pick him up at a motel he had rented. I slept there with him overnight. It was dingy and graffitied. The inside was crawling with cockroaches. Pepe made love to me with his wormy, warted member. It was uncomfortable and I just wanted to get it over with. Plus, I could smell the acne on his face as he kissed me.

We drove back to California that next morning. Pepe dominated the conversation as usual. He could talk non-stop for hours about inane things. Mostly, he would repeat the same stories from his past over and over again. I eventually learned how to drown him out.

My pimple prince, being thirty six and unencumbered by a car, had my grandfather drive him from music store to music store looking for a job. Finally, he was offered one in bike riding distance. We were only a few paychecks away from gaining our own place.

Pepe and I went out to the cantina to celebrate his new job. We stuffed ourselves on happy hour tacos and two dollar margaritas. We decided to take a night stroll on the beach, after a quick stop at the liquor store, of course.

Hand in hand, we walked with our feet in the water. It was a beautiful night, the moon was full. You could see far out into the tide. In the distance, you could hear the grunting of the sea-lions.

Suddenly, Pepe dropped my hand, "Oh, my God!" he screamed as he went running towards a group of rocks. He began climbing them as he looked out onto the waves.

"There it is! Do you see it? It's coming towards us, it's gonna' to kill us! We need to get out of here!" he shouted.

"Huh? What? Get off the rocks, what are you talking about?"

"Look!" Pepe pointed out into the water.

I didn't see anything, except, maybe a boat in the distance. Then another grunt from a sea-lion echoed through the shore.

"Follow me!" he ordered jumping off the rock and running in the direction of the street.

I just stood there confused.

"It's a fucking sea monster, *****! It's coming to the shore to get us!"

I started laughing, Pepe was hilarious.

He did not like this. Pepe was serious.

"You stupid bitch, are just going to stand there and be killed or what?"

"Pepe, there is no such thing as sea monsters."

"It's a giant octopus, like in the Popeye movie! I'm out of here."

Wanting to avoid an argument, I followed Pepe back to my car and drove us home.

We were having dinner with my grandparents the next night when Pepe decided to tell them about our little beach adventure. My grandfather, hard of hearing, just smiled and nodded. Grandma pulled me aside after and told me that she thought maybe Pepe had suffered some irreversible brain damage from all the drugs he probably did in his twenties.

As the days passed, Pepe and I started apartment hunting.

"The apartment has to be upstairs. Make sure the doors have dead bolts. If it's not secure people will break in and kill us," he warned.

Eventually I found the perfect place, Pepe did the safety inspecting. Though it did not meet his approval, he was ready to get out of my family's house and into a place where he could smoke pot freely. Pepe decided the apartment was good enough as long as he could install an alarm system and double-sided dead bolts.

I was soon reminded of why I left Pepe in the first place, living with Crater Face was not fun. He was very jealous and wouldn't let me go anywhere alone, I wasn't allowed to have friends over nor talk on the phone. As a matter of fact, if a man even looked at me in Pepe's presence, he would start a fight with him. Also, I was quickly growing bored with Puss Bubble's same seven stories.

As a means of escape, I started to stay late at work. The receptionist and I grew quite a bond and would stay after closing and share bottles of cheap wine. It was nice having someone to "girl talk" with.

One evening, after such a night, I ventured home relaxed. I made my way into the kitchen and started preparing Pepe's dinner as usual.

"What the fuck are you doing?"

"Making dinner, I thought we would have spaghetti."

"I mean why the hell are you home so late? It's six fifteen and I know your shop closes at five."

"Yah, I had a glass of wine with America."

"You are a fucking liar, you were out with a man. You were fucking some guy, weren't you?"

Pepe's eyes were twitching, violently.

"No, you dumb ass! I was having a fucking drink with my friend."

"You stupid, fucking slut! You think I don't know what you are doing? You think I'm dumb?"

Pepe slapped me across the face, I did not like this. I pulled out a kitchen knife and pointed it at him.

"Get the fuck out, Pepe. You are an insecure asshole."

Pepe stormed out, I could hear him slam the door. With tears streaming down my face, I continued to cook dinner.

He came back fifteen minutes later stinking like weed.

"I'm sorry," he said, "Were you really with America and not with a man?"

"Yes," I answered shortly.

"I shouldn't be so jealous. It's just that I have had girls cheat on me before. You are way out of my league."

I made both of us plates of food and handed Pepe his before having a seat at the table.

"You made this for me?"

"Yes."

"After what just happened? You still made me dinner?"

"Ya, I was cooking when it happened."

Pepe set his plate down on the table and pushed it away, "I'm not eating this. You fucking poisoned it! You are trying to poison me. You think I'm fucking stupid!"

I rolled my eyes and switched him plates. Then, I opened some wine.

Pepe started telling me all about his story "number four."

Once the wine had kicked in, I was feeling a bit chatty myself. Actually, I was feeling a little flirty. I pushed my little puss ball onto the floor and started nibbling his neck. I reached into his pants to feel him getting hard, my finger got stuck for a second, on the wart.

"Wanna' get some rug burn, Baby?" I asked him.

"I want to bend you over the couch!"

I giggled, "Okay!" before assuming the position. Pepe slapped my ass.

"I bet I'm the first guy to bend you over like this, aren't I?"

I started laughing, uncontrollably. I told you Pepe was hilarious.

"Ya, okay, Pepe!"

HAHAHAHAHAHAHA!

Pepe went soft, "Why is that funny? You think it's funny that you were a giant whore before you met me? You think I want to date some tramp who's fucked everyone in town?"

"You are stupid, you knew what I was before you committed."

"No, I had no idea what a slut you were."

With that, Pepe knocked me onto the floor. I pulled myself up and I shoved him back. Pepe did not like this. He threw a glass ashtray at me before forcing me back down to the floor. After he put his knees on my shoulders, he grabbed me by the cheeks. Then, he began slamming my head onto the ground. My head was making a loud "thump," my brain was bouncing around like a ping-pong ball. I twisted my body and kicked my legs but I couldn't get away. So, I started screaming.

"Help! Someone help me! Call 911! He's going to kill me!"

Pepe put his hand over my mouth. I bit him. That's all I remember.

When I came to, the police were there. Pepe was already in the squad car and I was being presented with papers.

"Ma'am, are you okay? Do you want to press charges?"

"Yes," I told the officer, as I signed the paperwork.

I didn't see Pepe again until a week later when he came to retrieve his belongings.

I already told you that story.

Piss & Shout

I had only been released from the juvenile slammer a few hours prior. My friend Elm pulled her car into my driveway and waited for me to climb inside before driving us out into the heart of Las Vegas. We were sixteen years old and on a mission to see our mutual friend, Sally.

We arrived to Sally's rundown apartment complex and parked. As I unbuckled my seatbelt, I noticed my boyfriend Sandman's baby blue, classic car parked in her lot. That mother fucker! What was he doing here? Elm saw the car too.

"Umm, *****, did you know that Sally and Sandman were hanging out today?" Elm asked me.

I shook my head. We walked to the front door and knocked. Laughter was emanating from the inside. A moment later, Sally turned the door knob and peered out. Her hair was disheveled and her lipstick was smeared. I looked inside to see her lipstick all over Sandman's ugly face.

"What is going on?" I asked Sally.

"Nothing, we were just hanging out. I thought you were still in juvie."

"No, I was released this morning."

"What the hell is that?" Elm asked pointing to a huge frame on the wall.

We all looked up. Hanging on the wall of Sally's mom's apartment was a giant, poster-sized portrait of Sandman. There he was, in all his gapped-tooth glory, with his long greasy hair wearing a ripped heavy metal band T-shirt, framed in 24×36. It was one of the oddest things I had ever seen.

Sandman started to explain about the picture but I had already had enough of the moment, I wasn't listening. I was pissed, shocked, and brokenhearted at catching him cheating on me. Not just cheating on me, but with my friend.

I stormed out the door and directly across the parking lot to Sandman's hunk of scrap metal. After violently pulling on the handle, I found it unlocked. Promptly, I slipped down my panties and climbed inside.

Popping a squat right on the drivers seat, I released a personalized river of vagina-ade. I could hear it as it streamed down the seat and onto the floor mats. It even had the distinct stench of the garlic lunch I had eaten earlier in the day. The more my bladder drained, the bigger the smile on my face became. Elm had followed me out and was laughing hysterically while still keeping watch.

"Oh, shit! Sandman is coming, run!" Elm screamed.

I looked to my right and there he was running towards me. As fast as I could, I jumped out of his piss-mobile with my panties still down around my knees. As I was running, I attempted to pull them up while peering behind me.

"Watch out!" Elm shouted once again.

I turned my head to look in front of me.

BONK!

I slammed face first into a pole. The blunt force dropped me to the ground, my bare bottom was skinned by the asphalt. Elm had her car idling as I picked myself up and jumped inside, bruised and bleeding.

As we were pulling away, I reached my hand out of the window and gave Sandman a nice look at my giant, middle finger.

A half-hour later, we reached Elm's house. She was still cracking up, she thought this was the most hilarious thing she had ever witnessed. Elm quickly decided that she had to brag about our escapades and called up our mutual bisexual friend, Queermy.

Queermy and I had dated several months prior. He had long black hair and wore fishnet stockings with twenty-eye combat boots and shorts. I thought he was a hot stud. He was my first bisexual (oh, how I love them) as well as the first man I ever had a clash of narcissism with.

MEOW!

Unfortunately, like many men I have dated in my past, the crush eventually turned into a rivalry.

"Queermy, you won't believe what ***** just did! She caught Sandman cheating on her with Sally, so she hopped into Sandman's car and she pissed in it!"

"No she didn't."

"Yeah, she did."

"Bullshit."

Elm handed me the phone, "Queermy thinks I'm full of shit," she said, "You tell him."

"Hello?" I said.

"What do you want?"

"I pissed in Sandman's car!"

"Yeah, right. Like I would believe that. You couldn't pull that off. You aren't cool enough."

"Yes I did! I even flipped him off as we were pulling out."

"No, you didn't. You are fantasizing about what you wish you would have done. Why don't you just admit you cried all the way home like the little bitch you are?"

"Fuck you! I did, too, piss in his car. If you don't believe me, I'll come piss in your house right now."

"You are such an idiot." he sighed, "If you even showed up here, I wouldn't open the door for you."

"Well, then I would piss in your bedroom window."

"No, you wouldn't, because you are a sorry little bitch. You are wasting my time, I'm busy watching commercials. I gotta' go."

CLICK.

"Elm, He seriously doesn't believe me!"

"I totally think you should piss in his window. That was a dare."

"That was a dare! You are right. How will I get my pee inside his window, though?"

Elm began looking around the room. She handed me a plastic cup.

"Perfect!" I agreed, "Give me some water, I need to fill my bladder back up."

Thirty minutes and four glasses of water later I felt it, that sweet urge to tinkle. I went into Elm's bathroom and pretended I was giving a sample at the free clinic. I filled that baby all the way to the top with my steaming waste concoction.

We headed back to Elm's car. Just as I grabbed the handle and opened the door, she cried out, "STOP! You are

NOT holding that cup in my car, it could spill! I don't want my car to stink like Sandman's."

"Please, Elm, his car probably stinks like garlic from my lunch, this batch is mostly water."

"NO! Roll down the window and keep your arm OUTSIDE!" she ordered.

I did as instructed and we were off, slowly. It was the first time in my life I was not scared of Elm's driving. Not to say that Elm was a bad driver in particular, but she is a woman.

Soon, what was destined to happen did. Elm went over a bump and the musty liquid contents of the cup splashed out and soaked my hand. No matter! The cup was still half full. See? I have always been an optimist.

We pulled up to Queermy's rotting shack and sure as shit, that fucker's bedroom window was wide open. Trying my best not to uncontrollably laugh, I crept out of the car with my cup in hand. Just as I took my body potion and splashed through his window, Queermy came running out of the house with a container of his own.

"OH CRAP!" I shouted.

"Damn right, oh crap!" he yelled back just as he released the contents of the bucket over my head.

It was cold.

I jumped into Elms car and she sped off.

"What did he throw on you? I almost left you, you know. It better not be pee!"

I sniffed my hair, it did not smell like anything.

"It was only water," I told her with a smile.

"You threw piss in his window! We drove five miles with it hanging out of the side of the car and all he had to counter with, at HIS OWN HOUSE, was water? What a loser."

We pulled into Elm's driveway and then walked inside. I passed by her brother and was just heading towards the bathroom to wash my pee-pee off of my hand when it happened. Elm had a flicker of genius and decided to seek a simple revenge.

"*****, stop for a minute. I don't think you have met my brother before, have you?" she asked me.

"No, I have not."

"Oh, well then *****, I would like you to meet my brother, Alvin."

Alvin looked at me with a twinkle of lust in his dweeby eyes.

Oh brother.

Pun, intended.

"Alvin this is my great friend, *****. Say hello, shake her hand."

Without a second thought, he reached his nerdy and blistered (probably from too much self-love) hand out, excited by the fact that he had just been given the chance to touch me.

With a smile that trembled from holding back roaring laughter, I grasped his hand. It took every ounce of strength in me not to piss my pants right there. I was lucky my bladder had been recently emptied.

I gave his paw a sturdy shake, then turned and finally made my way into the bathroom. In the distance, I could hear Elm shout out, "Wait, are you sure you want to wash it? Because I have a few more people I would like you to meet first!"

I flipped her off before shutting the door.

Demented Cheeto

One morning, while in my early twenties, I awoke in a dark and dehydrated hangover fog. Rolling my lumpy ass out of bed, I peered out the bedroom window. I couldn't recall the drive home from the night before, but my car was there, thank goodness.

Wait a second! I looked again, something was wrong. Yet, I couldn't quite place just what it was, considering how many brain cells were missing that morning. Then I realized it. My passenger side mirror was gone.

"That's shitty," I thought to myself and threw on a robe before venturing down to the front stoop. Once outside, I noticed my car was not in my usual parking spot. Just then, my grandpa walked out, "Parked on the lawn again, I see. Someone must have been drunk."

"I was not drunk, I was just tired," I lied.

Grandpa did not believe me.

I slowly stepped over to the passenger side to examine the damage. There was a yellow paint streak. Ugh, I needed a drink.

I got dressed and slapped on some make up. Then, I stopped at the corner store for a few bottles of cheap wine.

Next, I called Red, "Hey, Red," I greeted her quickly, "What are you up to today? I got shit faced last night and hit something, my car mirror is missing."

Red laughed. She was enjoying this, "What did you hit?" she asked.

"I don't know, Red! I was drunk! There is yellow paint on my car. Oh, God! Do you think I killed someone?"

Sweat would have been dripping down my forehead at this point, had I any fluids left in my dried out body.

Red laughed some more, "If you hit someone there would be blood on your car, not paint."

She had a point.

"Oh, my God, Red! I bet I took out a taxi! What if the police are looking for me?"

Red was laughing so hard by now, she probably pissed herself, "*****, if you hit another car, don't you think there would be more damage? Chill out. You probably backed into a pole pulling out of a parking spot."

Red is the smartest girl I know. This made me feel much better. However, I still needed a drink.

"What are you doing today?" I asked her, "I need a drink!"

"I'm heading over to Iggie's, meet me there."

"I'm already in the car and I have wine! I'll be there in fifteen minutes."

"Perfect!"

Fifteen minutes later, I parked in front of Iggie's house. I pulled my heavy-hangover-having, whore-ass out of the car. With wine in hand, I knocked on the door, Iggie answered. Her hair was wet and she was still in her pajamas.

"Hey, you!" she said, "Red was just on her way over."

"Yes, I know. She already told me. I brought wine. Glasses?"

"In the kitchen, that's just for you guys. Don't pour me any, it's way too early for me."

"What? Too early? It's almost noon! What's wrong with you?" I scolded her.

Just then, in walked Red. I poured each of us a glass. We all lit cigarettes and had "girl talk" for five hours, before finishing up the wine. Red walked to the store to buy some more.

She was taking a long time, too long. My buzz had more than kicked in, I was feeling a lot better now. Successfully, I had drunk my hangover away. I thought it would be hilarious to greet Red at the front door, when she came back, naked!

I would hug her.

Iggie, however, did not find my plan as amusing as I did. She was grossed out and a little scared. I laughed at her uncertainty. Once my clothes were flung away, I crept over to the door to wait. A few minutes later, Red entered. I lunged at her and grabbed her from behind.

"What the fuck?" Red screamed.

"*****! Jesus! Get away from the door, the neighbors will see you!" Iggie yelled out.

I laughed because I didn't care if they did, I was having an amazing time. My titties were flopping all around.

"Why is she naked?" Red asked Iggie.

"I don't know. You know very well that I can't handle her alone. Please stop leaving me with her when she gets this way."

This was hilarious.

Red poured me more wine. I sat back on the couch, naked, and lit another cancer stick.

We started discussing Iggie's current love interest as they tried to ignore my continuing nudity. I didn't care, I was having a great ole time.

"I fucking hate him, Iggie! He is nothing to me. He is less than nothing. He is smaller than small. Small like what is in his pants, like his little, baby nuts! That's right! He's like a nut, a pine nut! His nuts are smaller than pine nuts, even. They are currently dissipating into thin air as I speak. I'm gonna' eat that stupid pine nut in a salad. Then, I'm gonna' shit him out and I'm gonna' spit on him!" I loudly slurred.

Red got out her note pad. She was documenting my drunken quotes. This was amusing her. Even though she wasn't acting like it, Red was just as heavily intoxicated as I was.

"'Dissipated' is quite a large word for somebody so inebriated to be using," Iggie stated. I had impressed her with my vocabulary, even though I was still naked.

"I know, right?" Red agreed, "It's classic!"

"Really, I would prefer if you did not sit on my couch naked, *****. I do my work on that cushion and I don't want to be writing a report while sitting on your cooch crust," Iggie lectured.

"There won't be a mess, Iggie, she's got a tampon in. Look at the string!" Red pointed out.

We all looked down at the string.

Wait a minute, I hadn't put in a tampon that day. Where did it come from? I was really confused. Finally my memory made the connection, I had put it in the previous night, before my date and must have forgotten about it.

Hey, this meant I didn't put out after all! What luck! I didn't have to worry about getting another AIDS or pregnancy test right away. Sweet.

I figured I had better remove it. It had been there a long time and I wasn't in the mood to contract Toxic Shock Syndrome.

I reached right down into my furbie and pulled that baby out, holding it up in the air while examining it.

My friends screamed. It smelled.

"What does this look like?" I asked, hysterically laughing. The tampon was dangling from its string like a pendulum.

"Get that sick thing out of my living room, right now! Go, flush it! FLUSH IT!" Iggie demanded. She was actually really upset with me and my dangler.

Red had her hand over her mouth, she was leaning against the front door, laughing, "Holy shit! That is so gross! What's wrong with the color, why is it orange?"

"It's a demented Cheeto!" Iggie spat out.

They both still talk about this, I traumatized them for life. Also, I must admit I'm still a bit ashamed.

Kitty, Kitty Gang Bang

When people ask me the generic question, "What's the craziest thing you have ever done?" I just sit there and stare blankly at them. I mean, I never know how to respond to that. This story may be the answer. Another classic tale from the year I turned twenty one. Enjoy.

I was dating Stilts at the time. The company Stilts worked for flew him out to Chicago for a week on business. Stilts asked me to tag along.

We flew out of LAX on a Tuesday morning. This was just a few months after 9/11, so, we made sure to arrive at the airport three hours early in preparation for our flight. We waited for most of the time in line at the security gate. Already, we were fighting.

Yes, I was a loose, drunken skank. However, Stilts was a cheap, selfish asshole. He made plenty of money but insisted that I pay for my half of dinner when dining out. Plus, Stilts was always telling me what was wrong with me, he was obviously blind to the fact that I'm perfect.

Stilts and I arrived in Chicago and took a cab to our hotel room. He went straight to work while I watched daytime television in bed and ordered room service.

That evening we went out to a club. There was a dance contest. I entered and won an autographed CD. The DJ presented it to me. He thought I was cute so he bought me a drink. After, I introduced him to Stilts.

The DJ's name was Kitty. This was fitting considering that he was wearing cat ears on his head and had whiskers drawn onto his cheeks. He was tall with neon red hair. Also, he was a bisexual.

Kitty told Stilts and I about a loft party in a high rise. He would be DJing there later in the week and invited us to go. We said "maybe," having just arrived in town and not wanting to make any commitments quite yet. I put his number in my cell phone just in case.

The following night Stilts did not feel like going out, he was too tired so I ventured into the city alone. I went to a small bondage club that I had researched before the trip. My sexy self was wearing a short, low cut, black vinyl dress, fishnet stockings and eight inch stripper heels.

I walked inside the bar, lit a cigarette and ordered a drink. The bartender mixed it before handing it to me. While reaching into my pocket book for my money, he stopped me and then pointed to the ground, to my right.

Immediately, I looked down. That's when I saw it. No, it wasn't another midget, what's wrong with you?

It was a black man in bondage gear, he had on leather pants, a dog collar and black combat boots. He was on his knees with his mouth wide open and his hands folded behind his back.

In confusion, I looked to the bartender for an explanation. He just shrugged and walked away. Great.

The man spoke, "Excuse me, madam, but I would like the honor of buying your drink. I will also continue to cover the costs of all you can consume tonight. There is just one thing I will ask of you in return. In exchange for my generosity, I would like to be your 'human ash tray,' your 'slave' for the evening, have you will."

That was fucking weird. Let us take a moment to discuss this. The first problem I was having was the whole black/slave thing. I mean, come on! That's just messed up no matter how you look at it. Next, he wanted to eat my cigarette ashes. I am not going lie to you, I didn't even care about that part.

I reached my cigarette holding arm above my slave and ashed right into that maniac's mouth.

He really loved this, I wanted free drinks. I decided to get over the black thing right away.

Slave started to say something to me. The club was loud and I was already sure that I wasn't going to fuck him, so, I told him to shut the hell up. He listened and continued to buy me drinks as promised.

I slid off the bar stool and took a walking tour around the club. As I entered the adjoining dark room, I noticed that pushed against an even darker wall was a giant wooden cross with thick leather straps attached to it. The room was steamy and clouded from the fog machine.

Standing next to the cross, holding a leather whip was my new friend, Kitty. What luck? Kitty was excited to see me too. He hugged me hello.

"Good to see you! Where is Stilts?" Kitty asked me.

"Stilts was too tired to come out. He works again at five tomorrow morning," I answered.

Then, Kitty noticed Slave.

"I see you have already met Slave," Kitty said, "He's here almost every week. Is he bothering you?"

"No, it's OK. He's buying me drinks!" I said.

"Not anymore. I am."

With that, Kitty released Slave. Slave was a little disappointed but moved on to the next dumb slut, anyway.

"Who will be going up on the cross tonight?" I asked.

"You game?" Kitty smiled.

"Hell, ya!"

Let me stop here for a moment. Now, I know this may seem weird to some of you reading about this for the first time, but listen, I was into the bondage scene. I went to these clubs all the time back then.

I took off my dress and rested it on the back of a chair leaving on a black lace bra, thong panties, fishnets and my monster heels. Kitty took my hand and helped me onto the step. He pressed my chest against the cross and tied me against it with the leather straps. Then that man, again wearing his fuzzy, leopard print, cat ears, whipped my ass. Literally.

That's right, he pounded me with his leather paddle. I deserved this.

The spanking continued for a half-hour or so before we danced the night away. As the night wound down, we chatted. Kitty did not like that Stilts was leaving me alone in a hotel room all day long, he thought I needed some company. He said he would come visit me the following day.

When the club was closing, kitty called me a cab and promised to visit me after I had gotten some sleep.

Once back to the hotel room, I passed out. I don't even remember Stilts leaving for work, I just remember the knock on the door. It was around noon. My head was pounding, my ass was tender and purple from all the spankings. Literally, my mouth had dried shut. Once I grabbed a bottle of water, I walked over to the door in my thong panties and looked through the peep hole.

It was Kitty, I opened the door and he walked inside. He had something in his hand. Some sort of suction machine with tubes and cups attached. I had never seen anything like it before.

"What the hell is that?" I asked him.

"It's for fun," Kitty grinned.

Then he took off his pants and pushed me onto the bed. I got under the sheet, Kitty did too. He pressed his lips against mine.

All of a sudden, the handle to the front door turned. In walked Stilts. There we were, Kitty and I in bed together. Only Stilts didn't get it, I'm serious. He didn't have clue what was going on. Kitty was still wearing his shirt and I had on my bra. We were both nude under the sheet from the waist down. The TV was still on from the night before.

Stilts didn't even notice the torture device on the floor. He sat on the bed to the right of me. I was in between the two of them, I loved this.

"Hey dude! How's it going?" Stilts asked Kitty.

"Pretty good man," Kitty responded, "I just stopped in to say hi and bring you guys a flier to that loft party I told you about."

Then, I felt it. Kitty's hand was under the covers, he slowly moved it up my thigh and into my panties. He began finger banging me.

"Work let me out early today. The computers were down, can you believe it?" Stilts explained.

Oh, my God! I didn't know what to do. Then, a Christmas miracle occurred, Stilts got up to take a piss.

Once he shut the bathroom door, I pushed Kitty off the bed and slapped his hand. Kitty was proud of himself, he was laughing hysterically.

"Get out of here!" I hissed.

"No way! Then, Stilts will know for sure something is up. I can't believe he didn't say anything!"

"Get the fuck out!"

I finally pushed Kitty out the door, along with his box-o-doom.

Two days later Stilts had finally finished his work. We were flying home early the next morning. Stilts suggested, as to conclude the trip, that we attend Kitty's loft party that night. I always liked going to parties. I was in.

The loft was huge. All the walls and windows were covered with black paper. There were red lights flashing in time to the thumping beat of the music.

In the middle of the gigantic wall was a make-shift DJ booth. At the booth spinning, was our friend, Kitty. Once again, he had his cat ears on. Although, this time, he was dressed like a clown, a female clown. On his feet were a pair of floppy orange shoes, white face makeup and an orange, foam nose.

I greeted the circus creature before grabbing drinks and hitting the dance floor.

Next it was time to break the seal, I looked for the bathroom. There was a huge line. It was taking forever, I was ready to piss myself. I needed a plan.

I walked up to the first poor bastard in line. He was a heavy man in his early thirties, I smiled at him and he smiled right back.

"Listen," I said, "This is a loft space, and I know there is probably a shower in there. I am about to urinate on the floor. Is there any way you would consider letting me go in the bathroom with you to tinkle in the shower? I promise not to look."

As it turned out, the man's girlfriend was right behind him, she was also extremely intoxicated. She thought this was hilarious, also, brilliant. Actually, she couldn't wait any longer to go herself. She went into the bathroom with us and pissed in the toilet, making her guy use the sink at the same time I squatted in the shower.

We pee-pee tag-teamed.

Other people in line liked this idea, too. As a matter of fact, the line continued pissing in groups. I've always been a trend setter. There had to, seriously, had been close to twenty people in line for one shitter. It was a killer (clown) party.

Once my bladder was relieved, I looked around for Stilts. I could not find him but I didn't care. He had been annoying me all night, anyway. I had been enjoying my space away from him.

So, since it was my last night in the windy city and I was a shit-wrecked, psycho whore, I crawled under the DJ booth, lifted up Kitty's clown skirt and made his umbrella magically disappear.

That's right, I sucked off Kitty, the cross dressing clown, under a table while he had been spinning for a party my boyfriend had been attending.

Yup, I did that.

I even finished him off.

After I had devoured his clown nectar, I crawled out from under the table and guess who was standing right there?

Stilts. Uh huh, and he still had no clue what had just happened.

"Where were you? This party blows. Let's go back to the hotel," he ordered.

"Fine, let me say bye to Kitty."

I had just walked up to Kitty to say goodbye when I received the next surprise.

Kitty leaned in as he hugged me and whispered quickly into my ear, "I'll pick you up from the hotel in an hour. I'm going to take you home to meet my friend to....."

Kitty had just invited me to my very first two guy/one girl threesome.

Much like all young girls do, I had fantasized about this very situation since I was old enough to reach orgasm (fourteen if you were wondering). Kitty was about to make my dreams a reality.

I left the party with Stilts. Once we got in the cab, I picked a fight with the dumb bastard. That's right, I argued with him for exactly one hour. Then, I said I would meet him at the airport the next morning and stormed out with my luggage.

I walked through the hotel lobby and down the front entrance not a second too soon. Kitty had just pulled up. The passenger door of his car opened and a sexy, long haired, tattooed (you know my type already by now, don't you?) man let me inside the car. It was a bench seat.

I was already the cream filing of the cookie. Oh my, I was so excited! My panties are wet right now just thinking about it.

Once we arrived to Kitty's apartment, I was stripped, spanked and hand cuffed to the bed. I had man parts flying all around me. Kitty's pink, clown car took a spin. It entered the back seat of my love tunnel. Mike's meat stick was not far behind. It was coming for me....

...and then.......plooooooop.

Just as fast as it had arrived, it exited the station. Single, most disappointing moment, of my life. Mike had stage fright. That's right, and he never recovered.

The sun had just started to come up when Kitty drove me back to the hotel. Being a gentle-clown, he carried my luggage to the elevator. We stepped inside and I pushed the button for the fourteenth floor. That's when I heard it.
Kitty farted.
"Excuse me," he whispered obviously embarrassed, or maybe not, because then, Kitty farted again. Only this time he said nothing. Actually, Kitty continued to blow ass the entire fourteen floors! My disappointment had turned into disgust as I was trapped in an elevator full of smelly circus helium.

I began thinking to myself, "This is probably how those circus freaks get their tents to stay up," "That is probably what those huge balls used for balancing elephants are filled with," "I bet those circus assholes blame the smell on the monkeys."

I ran out of the rotton elevator and back to the room just in time to catch Stilts. We didn't speak the entire eight hour trip back.

I hung out with Stilts a few years after this all happened and I confessed the truth to him over some wine. He didn't believe me.

Grossest elevator ride, ever.

Doctor Headlock

I threw on a skanky pair of daisy dukes and packed an overnight bag full of the sluttiest little dresses I owned. Once my purse was flung onto my shoulder, I slipped on a pair of six inch stilettos and jumped into my little red station wagon. Las Vegas, here I come!

Finally, after a long hard year my big day had arrived. That's right, my divorce from Beans was becoming official. I had dreamed of this very day for so long. As a matter of fact, I'm pretty sure had my first fantasy on our wedding night, while we weren't having sex.

After I reached the interstate, I felt a wave of excitement hit me, in my panties. I didn't know if it was the release of all the marriage stress, the vibrations of the car or the way my shorts wedged against my clitoral piercing but right there, next to a van carrying a large Asian family, I orgasmed. Without ever having touched myself.

It was magical.

Once I arrived into town, my first stop was the hotel room. I changed into something more appropriate and headed out to retrieve my freedom. Next stop, mediation.

It was a hot summer day. Beans had not laid his dumb eyes on me in several months. I was no longer a fatty. We sat down on a bench outside together and smoked cigarettes awaiting our turn.

"You have lost weight," Beans stated this newfound knowledge as if he was a genius, "Looks good."

"Thanks."

Moron.

After a good half hour of uncomfortable small talk, it was time. Together we walked into mediations. I paid the fee of one hundred dollars. Beans paid nothing because he was still out on disability.

"Hello. My name is Darla," the counselor began in the most monotone voice I had ever heard, "I will be your counselor. Let me explain how mediations will proceed. Each of you will get a chance to talk to me 'privately,' while the other waits outside. You can tell me 'privately,' what you each need to discuss with the other. Then we will all meet together and I will be here to assist should either of you need me....."

That bitch talked on for a good 15 minutes. I wasn't listening, I was having flash backs of my tire tickles from earlier.

Beans stood up and opened the door, it pulled me out of my fog. I was given the first turn. My concerns on the custody of my daughter were simple, education, sibling separation, her to have the right to a smoke-free house, having her own room and the female bond. I explained this to Darla in thirty seconds.

"Okay, well you can explain that to Beans, then," she said.

I walked out of the room, Beans entered behind me as I took a seat outside. He was in there for an hour. What the hell was he doing, getting a blow job? Really, I didn't care what he was doing, I was ready to sign those damn papers and get back to the hotel.

My Who Res' were throwing me a divorce party!

Finally, mediation began. As I had assumed, Beans didn't listen to any of my reasoning behind what I thought would be best for our daughter. He wanted to win and was prepared to bully me until I gave in. This was very annoying. I still find it extremely difficult to tolerate those with small intellects.

Beans continued to stand his ground like a big, dumb wounded Pit Bull until I agreed to disagree and fight it all out in court later. Darla sat there holding a stupid grin, completely useless.

We were going over possible meet up places for our legally ordered custody exchange. Beans decided I couldn't be trusted, even with a court order, and insisted we meet at the police station.

"Fine, I don't even care. We can picnic," I said.

That is when it happened, Darla started giggling. She put her hand over her mouth. Her eyes were sparkling like diamonds.

"I'm glad you find this amusing, Darla," I spat.

"I was just picturing you all at the police department, on the lawn, having a picnic. What a site that would be."

"Are you laughing at me?" I asked.

"No, just the comment..."

It felt like I had been sitting in a competition for the mentally challenged. I gave Darla a dirty stare. That bitch shut the hell up. I decided, much like Beans, she was useless. Before heading out I made sure to fill out a comment card, truthfully.

Party time!

Laverne pulled up to the hotel not a minute after I did, she brought with her, a case of beer. I love that bitch. We got dressed and I styled our hair in preparation of getting our buzz on.

Once we looked like giant sluts, okay, once I looked like a giant slut, we hit the casino floor. After several beers, rounds of cheap sparkling wine and the "burning away twenties in a machine" ritual, Tangerae' arrived. She wasn't alone! Our good friend Fiona was with her. Fiona was in town for the weekend too and decided to surprise us.

Yippee!

We threw more money away, drank more champagne and then Fiona said something that pissed me off.

I have no clue now what she said.

HA HA HA!

I decided to challenge her to a wrestling match. Fiona was a lot bigger than me, probably by a foot. Pure muscle.

However, I was drunk and sure that I could take her. We went back into the room and I went for that bitch.

In .01 of a second she had me in a head lock. I yelled uncle. Fiona let me go.

The minute that beastly bitch turned away, I went for her throat.

In .01 of a second, Fiona had me back in a head lock.

This time I put up a fight. I kicked and I squirmed but the ogre was not even fazed.

Tangerae' and Laverne loved this. I was a foot taller than both of them and for the entire fifteen years of our friendship, I had bullied them. They loved watching me get my ass smashed. I deserved this.

After five minutes of acting like a retard with a jar of hot sauce, I yelled uncle.

I needed a plan, I was going to use my drunken intellect. After a little blurry plotting, I decided I would trick Fiona into being friends again. Once we were friends she would let her guard down, then, I could finally take her out.

I opened Fiona a beer. She drank it and commented on how cute a pair of my shoes were, before trying them on. They fit her perfectly.

"Fiona, you keep the shoes. I bought them to wear to court today and the case is over, so I won't need them again."

"Really, are you sure?"

"Take them, Fiona!" Laverne chimed in, "***** only wears hooker heels, anyway. She won't ever wear those again."

Laverne looked over at me, "***** I'm shocked you even bought something that conservative to begin with!"

"Right!?" Tangerae' agreed, laughing, "***** dresses like a total whore!"

"Fuck you both!" I screamed, "I hate you!"

Fiona was busy putting on her new shoes when I saw my chance. I rushed at her and leaped right onto her warty back.

In .01 of a second, Fiona had me in a head lock.

Pissed and defeated by nine o'clock, plus already shit faced, I threw myself down on the bed to pout.

"Get up, *****," Tangerae begged, "Let's go back to the casino floor."

"NO! I'm tired," I whined like a child.

They all tried to get me up but I was done. I was starting to get the spins and light bruises were already forming all over my wimpy body. I passed out.

It was roughly four o'clock in the morning when I heard it, pounding on the hotel room door.

"*****, wake opp! Bitch! I know yooze arrrr in dare! I can heeer you!"

It was Laverne and Tangerae, they were still partying.

"O pan thesssss door, Beeech! Weeee brought yooze a doctor! Heeze focking single, Beeech, and hay wantssss to meet you!"

They went away after about ten minutes but the bruises lasted for weeks. Also, they still remind me about the hot doctor I missed out on.

Oh, well.

40's & Phone Balls

One evening, while sitting alone on the futon in my empty ghetto apartment, I was drinking my usual gallon of cheap merlot and feeling sorry for myself in front of some stupid reality show. Did I mention I was alone?

In those days, I was always lonely. Plus, I was bloated and puffy. After Pepe moved out I decided to keep the apartment we had shared. I did have my newly acquired, retarded dog with me but she was more of an annoyance than a companion.

Literally, I drank on thirty pounds. I looked like a marshmallow, if marshmallows had crusted red wine lips.

One evening while drowning in my own misery it happened, the phone rang.

"Hello?" I answered.

"*****?"

"Yah......?"

"Hey, it's Tyler, Tyler Phillips. Haden gave me your numba'. Do you remember me?"

HOLY SHIT.

Tyler was the boy who beat me up in the 7th grade.

"Yes, I remember you. How are you these days?"

"I'm a'ight. Just left my old lady back in Montana. She left me for my best friend, dat dumb bitch. We have three girls (children) togetha', too."

"Wow. That's crazy! Where are you living now?" I asked.

"I'm at my mom's house in Las Vegas until I can get on my feet, I'm really missin' my girls. Hey, I just wanted you da know dat I'm sorry for what happened all those years ago. I always felt bad about what I did."

"What? That was so long ago, I barely remember it."

"Dat's not who I am anymo'," he said with a hint of black in his voice that was a little sexy. Actually, Tyler sounded just like a white rapper, only slower.

Tyler and I caught up. As a matter of fact, we talked for four hours. The next night we talked for five. Actually, we talked all night every night for a month. I couldn't wait for my work day to end so I could get home and call my little Trailer Tiger. We would watch TV and discuss the shows together. My loneliness had finally come to an end.

One night, roughly two hours into my and Tyler's evening talk, I did it. That's right, I suggested that he come down for a visit. I was curious to see how the years had treated my little Teen Dream, plus, I was horny.

Tyler did not have any money because he still didn't have a job. So, I offered to pay for his bus ticket, Tyler's mom, needing a break from her 25 year old baby, gladly offered to pay half. Tyler was coming into town the following weekend. I was so excited I could hardly contain myself. Though, I must admit that I was a little worried.

Finally, the big day arrived. I pulled into the Greydog station and parked before looking around, that is when I saw him. Just like in Jr. High, Tyler was wearing his red Starters jacket promoting his favorite team. I did not know they still made those kinds of jackets.

I waved to him with my floppy arm. My flabby, white legs were hanging out of my short skirt and platform shoes. We made eye contact and he came walking over to my car with a little gangster swag in his step. He opened the door and shoved his back pack in as I reached over and gave him a warm hug. When I let go of his neck he grinned and that's when I saw it.

Chipped front tooth.

Other than the obvious dental damage, Tyler was still pretty much a hottie. Long gone was his bowl cut, in its place a short, shaggy, crop cut that was long overdue for a trim. I would fix that. There, perched in the middle of his face, illuminating, were his giant, magnificent blue eyes. Still, he was a little trashy.

No matter, I had stocked my apartment with lots of wine for this very special occasion. If things turned out to be bad, I would just drink away the annoyance. We headed back towards my apartment.

"I hope you like merlot," I said.

"What's dat?" he asked.

"Merlot? It's red wine."

"Nah, I don't drink much wine except that box stuff my ma keeps around da house. I like fo-teez of malt lick-a. I can drank three or fo' of dose a day. But I guess if wine is all ya got den that's what all drank. I ain't got much money on me."

"Oh, well I will stop at the store, I'll buy you some beer. You are my guest after all."

"Aw, thank you. That's cool. You don't gots to do that."

Tyler and I stopped at the first liquor store we saw. We emptied out an entire shelf of forty-ounce beers.

Once back to my place we began our drinking. Somewhere around the tenth hour it happened, Tyler kissed me. I took off his pants. He had an enormous erection. There was something else in his pants that night too.

Giant rat nuts.

I'm serious! Have you ever contemplated the proportion of a male rat versus the size of his goat? It was like Tyler had two deflated hot air balloons hanging from the stem of his stick shift. Only, they were rubbery and a little wet. They felt like those sticky hands you bought out of the quarter vending machines as a kid but colder.

They caught hair and lint pretty much in the same fashion, too. I had that retarded dog that shed everywhere. This was very gross, when I went down on Tyler, I came back up with chin hair.

Tyler penetrated me that night. His mammoth, vained, vermin testies flopped onto my knees and caught skin as he tried to grind back and forth on top of me. It was like getting a leg massage from a giant pancake.

I didn't really care though because I was drunken, lonely and desperate. That's right, I needed any man.

Even, a Rat Man.

Tyler was one of the horniest men I had ever known. Those rat sacs would fill right back up in a matter of minutes.

He pounced on me three more times that night. We spent the rest of the weekend drunk and naked covered in dog hair.

The following Sunday, hung-over and chafed, I was sad to see Sir Dicks-a-Lot go. I was once again forced to return to my loneliness. With tears in my booze swollen eyes, I left him at the bus depot.

He called me that evening when he returned to his mom's house. We talked our usual marathon.

After we hung up, I made my decision, I did what any stupid, self-loathing sociopath would do, I decided I was going to ask my little love rodent to move in with me.

Of course, that's another story.

Mr. Personality

I was at the bondage club on my usual night with a group of friends when I walked out onto the patio to have a cigarette and scope out the leather clad hotties. That is when I saw him, sexy guy with dreadlocks. I shall call him, Mr. Personality.

We made eye contact and I smiled. This did not do the trick. He must have been shy. I put a cigarette in my mouth and clanked my 8 inch heel wearing, whore ass over beside him.

"Can I have a light?" I asked. Coversation initiated.

"You live around here?" he questioned, as he lit my cigarette.

"About 30 miles away. How about you?"

"Just down the street. We should hang out sometime, are you into art? I have two tickets to my friends play next weekend, if you want to go."

"I love art," I said as I giggled.

It was a date.

On the drive home, I told my friend Bella all about my new boy crush.

"He invited you to a play? Where is it at?" she wanted to know.

"In LA."

"Where does he live, is he picking you up?"

"No, he lives in LA, so I told him that I would meet him at the venue."

"Woa! No, way *****. On a first date, the guy always picks you up and you should not go into another city. He needs to meet you close to home," she lectured, "After all, he could be a serial killer!"

Bella had a point.

The night before our first date, when my rasta-gothian called me to confirm, I broke the news.

"Uh, I really want to hang out but I need to stay close to home. Can we do something in my area instead?"

"Oh, well I promised my friend...well...nothing, yes, I can come your way. That would be fine."

"Awesome, thanks! See you then," I hung up the phone.

That next evening I put on some music and blasted it at full volume while I whored myself up. I put on a short skirt, fish net stockings and red knee-high, platform boots. After two hours of slapping on the war paint, I saw lights radiate through my bedroom window, I looked outside to see Mr. Personality's car pull into my driveway.

Slowly, I crept to the front door and opened it with a giant grin on my face and the sexiest pose I could form.

"Hello there," I moaned in a sex kitten voice.

Mr. Personality looked at me and then he put his finger to his lips and hushed me. He was on the phone.

I left him there with the door open and went back inside to grab my bag. Once I returned to the porch he was off the phone, I followed him to his car.

"Where do you want to eat?" he asked me.

I gave him the rundown of the usual local joints and he picked one. Besides for me giving directions, we drove there in silence. Once we had arrived and he parked his car, we walked inside the restaurant together to be seated.

Mr. P looked over his menu before we ordered. He said absolutely nothing.

"So, how long have you lived in LA?" I finally asked.

After a moment of silence he responded with, "A year."

I could faintly hear crickets chirping.

"Do you like it?" I asked.

"Yes."

Mr. Personality was blankly staring at something behind me. I turned around, yet there was nothing there.

"Where are you from?" I tried again.

"Florida."

He looked at his watch.

Dread-silence.

I started to do what I do best and ramble on about how much I love myself and how cool I am but he was not listening.

I shut the hell up.

After what seemed like an eternity, the food was finally served. We ate without a word. As it turned out, Mr. Personality did not have one. Once we finished............

Wait a minute, hold up. I am SO BORED WRITING THIS STORY that I can't even think of anything witty to insert here, I'm falling asleep!

Anyway, after the stupid dinner, Mr. Personality drove us to a movie (you can see where this is going, right?). He paid for the tickets and we still had twenty minutes to kill so we sat down on a bench outside of theater 10, he said nothing to me. Sitting there silently, he continued to check his phone and watch a blank wall. I would have asked him to take me home if he hadn't been so good-looking. The time passed very slowly. Finally, it was time for the film.

Lamest movie ever.

I excused myself probably five times to go to the bathroom just for an excuse to walk around. The movie was two hours and fifty minutes long. When it finally ended my blah-date turned to me and said, "That movie sucked. I wanted to leave hours ago."

I just looked him in the eye and blinked, I wanted to slug him.

He drove me home. Probably, I fell asleep on the way.

Now this is where I wish that I didn't have anything to write about. I should have called it quits then. But no, his beauty outweighed my brains because I went out with him again a week later. It was less boring.

Since I was now convinced that my dead-locked hunk was not a murderer, I agreed to meet him for a movie at his place. He was an artist himself and as it turned out he lived in a very interesting loft in an even more captivating building. Actually, he was talented and his art kept me occupied.

We sat on his couch and watched a movie, quietly. Then, it happened. Rope Head kissed me. His lips were soft and his breath was sweet. Like the giant slut I was, it didn't take long before he had me on his bed. He pulled my dress over my head as I tugged off his pants. Once he had sufficiently teased me and I was rearing to go, he asked me the big question,

"Can I put it in your ass?"

I was not THAT rearing, "Woa! What? You want to do what?"

"Can I put my dick in your ass. Come on, you will like it, trust me. My ex did not like it at first but after a while, she learned to love it. You will too!"

Now, I was still only a half giant slut in those days because rear entry was not something I commonly practiced. Actually, I had only done it once before and that was by surprise. However, Mr. P was hot and he just said the magic words to me, "after a while." That's right, my boring prince was planning on keeping me around! Why, I wanted nothing more in the world than a serious relationship with someone. I guess if anal sex was what I had to do to get a boyfriend you could count me in.

"Okay," I said, "Be gentle."

He rolled me over onto my stomach and then began trying to put his member in my "member's only club." It hurt, I braced the head-board.

Then, I screamed, "Lube! We need lube."

Mr. Personality began looking around his room for something to smear on his dread cock. That is when I spotted it, hand soap.

I need not explain any further. Dumbest thing I have ever suggested, to this day.

Just writing this I can feel the sting. I would rather rub jalapeno in my eye or pour rubbing alcohol inside a stab wound.

In tears, I sprinted to his shower and ran water over myself for an hour until the pain became manageable. I drove home sitting on a jacket I had rolled up like a donut.

I farted bubbles for days.

I told myself that it would all be worth it because now I had my very own mute man.

I sent Mr. P an email a few days later. He responded and our conversation continued back and forth that week but he never mentioned going out again. So, one night, I figured I would ask him. We had had sex already, kinda. It was okay for me to start initiating the dates at this point. I mean, he was pretty much already my boyfriend.

"I can't wait to see you again, Stud," I emailed, "What are we doing this weekend?"

A few minutes later my phone rang. I looked at my caller ID. It was him!

"Hi," I said, my voice was filled with excitement.

"Hey, *****. I just wanted to call because I feel like I need to explain something to you."

"Sure," I said.

How sweet he already had emotions for me. Probably he was going to tell me how I needed to be gentle with his heart. I knew he had just come out of a serious relationship.

"I am not looking for a girlfriend right now, okay?"

CRUSH!

For once, I was the silent one.

"Ok," I eventually responded.

Then it happened, I could not believe it. Mr. Personality started talking. He talked to me for thirty, stupid minutes about his family and his school before hanging up.

He never called me again. Not for year anyway, but that's another story.

How I Shot Donut

Once this book was almost completed, I needed a cover. I was unemployed, obsessed with stardom and still in love with Donut. So, I planned a photo shoot, with lots of donuts.

First, I asked all my photographer friends if they would be interested in working with me. Then, I explained my ideas, to be naked and covered in donuts. That's right, as a tribute to my little cream puff. I found one friend, Phog, who was willing to help me create my vision despite my obvious insanity.

Next, I was going to need an assistant, I asked my little Asian friend, Ha, for help. I do not know how I am always able to convince Ha into following my crazy schemes. Even though she was not looking forward to hanging with me outside all day while I was naked, she agreed. Probably out of pity. Her life must be really boring.

I needed money for the shoot, I decided I needed an investor. By investor, I mean donator and by donator I mean I went onto a sugar daddy website and told men to give me money. This worked. Turns out, wealthy men love to give money to hot, younger blondes for retarded projects. I told you, men are stupid.

I spent the few days prior to the shoot scoping out donut shops and I asked the shop owners what they did with their donut surplus at the end of the night. Perhaps I could purchase their old donuts before they threw them away.

They all said no. Donut selling Asians are stingy. I asked if they would grant me a discount if I bought in bulk.

One shop owner said, "No discount! Dah-knotts discounted already!"

I went ahead and bought out most of his donut store, anyway. When asked why I needed so many, I told him and his partner that the donuts were for a photo shoot and were to be destroyed. Then I handed them both my blog business cards.

The owner read one of them out loud, "'I hate dawgs, spess-ly wee-ta-ted wons! Also, I hate dah-knotts!' Oh, you no like dah-knotts?" he asked me.

"Donut is a man, I am going to smash them," I explained.

They both laughed very hard. I had amused them.

The morning of the shoot, I sent my family to an amusement park for the day as so I could utilize my grandma's backyard. This shoot was to be very messy.

Guess what? Donuts made for some creative costume ideas. I made a doughnut bikini, doughnut hole necklace, you name it. That's right, I even set up a staging area.

Ha showed up early to help decorate my naked body with frosting and sprinkles. She slapped the goo onto me, taking special care to cover up my problem areas. At first, Ha was embarrassed for me and a little disgusted. As the day went on, she started to get into the set design. She may have discovered her calling.

As the shoot progressed, I went through several different costume changes. I acted out the most disturbing, sexual things I could think up with the donuts. I am classy.

Ha was a natural, setting up my pastry props in ways to cover my "rated X" spots while Phog shot on.

"That donut on the crotch of your panties is disgusting!" Phog mentioned, "It seriously looks like you have a package."

"Perfect! Donut would like this, he's a bisexual," I replied.

Ha covered me in powdered sugar, strawberry jelly, heart confetti, you name it. I was a hot, sticky mess but I was having a blast. Pretty much, I am an all-around dirty girl.

Finally, it was time to film the video.

I decided that, in one of the scenes, it would be funny if I was hit in the face by a flying jelly doughnut. Ha was to chuck the donut at my face while Phog filmed. This brought Ha much satisfaction. She loaded that doughnut up with as much extra jam as she could squeeze into it and topped it with powdered sugar from a box. Then, she pitched it at my face like she was on a major league. We had to re-shoot this scene several times to get it right because I could not stop laughing. I deserved this.

My favorite scene was of my foot in a six inch, red stiletto, stomping a doughnut to death. It made me feel all warm and fuzzy inside.

The shoot was a success, though I do not know if either friend will ever hang out with me again.

Epilogue: Smart Whore

I have learned a lot of things through writing this book. Brutus may not have been the first man to use me, however he will be the last. It is amazing how much one can see of themselves by reflecting back through their own written word.

Today, I have decided to let go of some of the intimate details I had been keeping of Donut as I no longer want them. Your life will never be the same after reading this. You're welcome.

One weekend, roughly a month into our reunion dating, Donut sent me a text:
Donut: Have you ever tried poppers before?
Me: No, what's that?
Donut: Ammonium nitrate, look it up.
Me: Oh, my God! You want to blow me up?
Donut: Oops! I mean alkyl nitrite. No, it's safe.

After I conducted a quick internet search, I came to conclude that this was a gay thing. One of the many advantages of dating a bisexual is that they know about all the sick shit the gays do in bed too. Double kink, two for one.

Me: I don't know about that, sounds kinda' scary.

That was a lie, I would have done anything my little cream puff suggested. I really loved him. Probably, I would have let him kill me and then fuck my decaying corpse too, had he but asked.

Donut: Poppers come in a tiny jar, you sniff them and they relax your body while giving your brain a high. They are great for relaxing during anal sex.
Me: I'm down for anything you want to do sexually.

Donut: Really? I have always fantasized about eating another man's spooge out of a pussy.

Me: I know, I remember. Involving another person might not be the best idea, but I will if you want me to.
Donut: No, it's okay. You remember everything. How about I freeze my own cum and then eat it out of your pussy once it melts?
Me: Sure!
Donut: Really?

Donut just didn't get it.

The following Thursday finally arrived, I made sure I looked perfect. Every inch of my body was painted, prepped and groomed for my special love session with my puffed daddy. I had fantasized about being with him all week long. Anything that turned him on automatically turned me on, as well. For Donut, I had no limit.

As usual, I stopped at the grocery store on my way to pick up some beer and snacks. The clerk probably thought I was a hooker but I didn't care. Donut loved me dressed this way and I loved to please him. He still does not know that I like to hang out barefoot in my pajamas most of the time with un-manicured finger nails.

Ha!

I arrived at my dream shack around the same time as him. As usual, we engaged in our ridiculously humorous, fucked up in all ways conversation, drank beer and smoked cigarettes. Once the night began to get late, Donut passionately led me to his mattress of love.

He kissed me, touched my body and peeled up my dress. Then, he made sweet love to me until I reached orgasm.

Donut instructed me to get on "all fours." He stood up with his cock erect, and told me not to move, "Stay there! I'll be right back."

I did as my maple man instructed.

Donut strutted back into his bedroom and stood behind me, he began kissing the back of my neck. I loved this! Then, I felt something cold enter me. He had just inserted an ice cube of his semen inside my whore hole. This was not any normal shaped ice cube either. Donut had created this special specimen in a Halloween themed ice cube tray. That's right! It was shaped like a skeleton finger.

Zombie hand job.

His hard cock slipped into my pussy as he slowly mounted me. With one hand, he grabbed me by my hair.
With his other arm, he gently reached around my neck and placed a tiny bottle in front of my nose, the poppers. I breathed in the fumes. Almost immediately, I felt it. I started giggling. Donut huffed a little of his own. He continued to penetrate me as the ice cube of his manhood melted inside.
When he was close to the finish line, he delivered us each another sniff of the bottle before lying on the bed and pulling me on top of him, sixty nine. I put Donuts massive member inside my mouth, he shoved his tongue inside my sloppy sissy and then he finished in my face, we both swallowed.
Once it was over, Donut decided that I had not yet had enough of his Johnson juice, he grabbed me by my cheeks and kissed me. Very disgusting, we both gagged. Only, it was not disgusting because it was Donut.

He still dumped me.

I am on the market, men of the world, and I do sick shit like this. Probably, I am going to need to hire a bodyguard now.
I will see you all at the book signing!

xoxoxoxox

Acknowledgments

You guys are so damn awesome!

Thank you to everyone for reading this piece of filth and making my dreams of becoming a famous celebrity one step closer to a reality.

Special thanks to Red for helping me find a site to start my writing on and encouraging me all the way to pursue yet another one of my *horrible* ideas.

Pepper, without you none of my soul searching would have began and I would probably still be chasing Donut. Thank you from the bottom of my *rotting* heart.

Danielle Isme, thank you for listening and encouraging my art. Yet, not once calling me *crazy* to my face.

Shout out to Nicholas Iverson, for spending an entire afternoon with me in my backyard naked with donuts. Also, for editing out my *loose stomach skin*.

Sandy Khlok, it took *guts* to not spill yours while rainbow sprinkling me. Thanks for that, also for the endless hours of Donut tears you wiped away.

Brandi Whitehouse, thank you for making my photos pop and whoring out my horrible blog. Plus, the "*bird feeding*."

Voodooman93, for hearing my "cries." Also, *stranger pubes*.

Jenn Adams, for fighting Word on my behalf and *attempting* to fix my grammar.

Hugs to <u>DP</u> for helping me turn this *trash* into something (twice), you are the bomb.

To the rest of my <u>media whores</u>: Chere Fairchild, Bethany Wolfe, Andrea Rosen, Khira Howarth, Randyd Gonzalez, Romeo Razi (my first fan), Doug Baker, Kasey Shea, Edy Hansen, Scheryll Eddy, Sveta Chaynikova, Alisha Coppedge, Sanya Briggs, Milo Simmons, Lindsey Michelle Berman, Kathy Carver, Isis Magic, Michael Hage, Erica S. Finstad, Sonia Alva, Nathan Popejoy, Rudy Montanaz, Amanda McNamara, Raeann McNamara, Mindi Arrant Wamack, Joshua Paul Hawkins, Kimberly Nething, Anthony Vincent Garcia-Maestas, Dina O'Brien Button, Gary Tate and the rest of my online family. I apologize to those whom I have missed, I owe you a drink because I am an asshole.